CCtw
ɔ١٥

SECRETS

of the

CIRQUE
MEDRANO

SECRETS

of the
CIRQUE
MEDRANO

A novel by **Elaine Scott**

ini Charlesbridge

For Cindy and Susan, my daughters; my works of art. —E. S.

A writer always needs good friends who will listen and, when asked, offer advice. I had three good friends who helped me see this book to publication. First I would like to thank my dear friend, Diane Stanley, who encouraged me with "You can" when I was thinking "I can't." Next I want to thank my always-supportive agent, Susan Cohen, who looked at the manuscript and said "You did," and last, but certainly not least, my delightful and wise editor, Judy O'Malley, who said, "We will," and brought the book to publication. They were my lifelines.

Published by Charlesbridge
85 Main Street
Watertown, MA 02472
(617) 926-0329
www.charlesbridge.com

Library of Congress Cataloging-in-Publication Data
Scott, Elaine, 1940–
    Secrets of the Cirque Medrano / Elaine Scott.
        p. cm.
    Summary: In the Paris village of Montmartre in 1904, fourteen-year-old Brigitte works long hours in her aunt's café, where she serves such regular customers as the young artist Pablo Picasso, encounters Russian revolutionaries, and longs to attend the exciting circus nearby. Includes author's note on the Picasso painting *Family of Saltimbanques.*
    ISBN 978-1-57091-712-7 (reinforced for library use)
    1. Montmartre (Paris, France)—History—20th century—Juvenile fiction.
[1. Montmartre (Paris, France)—History—20th century—Fiction. 2. Paris (France)—History—1870–1940—Fiction. 3. France—History—Third Republic, 1870–1940—Fiction. 4. Restaurants—Fiction. 5. Picasso, Pablo, 1881–1973—Fiction. 6. Circus—Fiction. 7. Orphans—Fiction. 8. Europe—Politics and government—1871–1918—Fiction.] I. Title.
PZ7.S419Se 2008
[Fic]—dc22   2007002329

Printed in the United States of America
(hc) 10 9 8 7 6 5 4 3 2 1

Illustrations done in pastels on Canson paper
Display type and text type set in Mister Earl and Baskerville MT
Color separations by Chroma Graphics, Singapore
Printed and bound by Lake Book Manufacturing, Inc.
Production supervision by Brian G. Walker
Designed by Diane M. Earley

Chapter 1

THE TRIP

BRIGITTE DUBRINSKY was shaken out of an uneasy nap by the hiss from the steam engine and the protesting screech of the train's wheels on the track. With eyes only half-open, she absentmindedly reached up to straighten her kerchief. Next she tugged her thick braid of blond hair toward the center of her neck and smoothed the surface of the braid with her fingertips. Dropping her chin to her chest, she rolled her head from side to side to ease the burn in her neck and shoulders. She had been on the train for thirty-six hours, traveling from Warsaw to Paris—from the old life to the new.

As she raised her head and opened her eyes, a man sitting directly across from her held out a wrinkled piece of paper.

"I believe this may belong to you, Mademoiselle. It fell off your lap while you were sleeping."

Startled, Brigitte recognized the letter that had changed her life, and without thinking, she reached over and snatched it. As she did so, she felt her fingernail make contact with the back of the man's hand.

"Ow!" The stranger jerked his hand away, rubbing the back of it vigorously. Brigitte—cheeks burning and heart slamming—watched in horror as the thin red scratch that she had made began to appear.

As clearly as if her mother had been seated by her side, Brigitte's mother's voice echoed in her brain. "Child, will you ever learn not to be so impulsive? Think before you act."

Brigitte looked at the man and stammered, "I'm sorry, sir. I didn't mean to harm you, or to be so, so . . . rash. It's just that the letter is important. Here, take my handkerchief," she added, holding out a clean white square of linen.

"It's just a scratch," he said, waving away the peace offering. "But if that letter is important enough to inflict bodily harm on a person, then I'd take better care of it if I were you. Frankly, it looks rather tattered." He gave his hand a final rub, took a topcoat from the rack above the seat, and without looking in her direction again, joined the other passengers filling the aisle in anticipation of the train's final stop.

Brigitte was in no hurry to leave the train, so she remained seated, inspecting the letter. It was still intact. Only a corner had been torn off. By now she could have recited its contents from memory, but she smoothed its crumples with the palm of her hand and read it once again.

August 3, 1904
Paris
My dear Sandrine,

It grieves me to learn of your illness. Though we have been apart these years, you are still my little sister and I weep for you at this time. Tuberculosis is a terrible scourge. I have prayed for a cure. Had you not gone off to Poland, who knows how life would have turned out for you?

Georges and I have spoken about this situation and we are prepared to offer Brigitte a home with us. Our café is small, but more and more customers come. They are an interesting, but rather strange, group. At least all of them seem to like my cooking.

I am glad to hear that the priests at Saint Stanislaus have educated Brigitte. To have completed eight years of schooling is quite an accomplishment, and it pleases me to know she has had this advantage. However, now that her school days are over, she should think about a vocation.

We live above the café, and there is a small room where Brigitte will be comfortable and safe. And since Georges and I have never been blessed with children, it is possible that one day, if she works hard, the Café Dominique could belong to her.

When we arrange the date and time, tell her she is to wait on the platform after she leaves the train. She is not to move. We will find her after the crowd thins. After all, how many young girls could be standing alone on a train platform?

And now I commend your health into God's care.

Your sister,
Dominique Boudoin

Brigitte remembered the day she read the letter for the first time. She winced at her behavior as she recalled wadding it into a ball and throwing it across the room in a fit of temper—and fear. Fixing her gaze on her mother, she'd insisted, "I'm not going to Paris! I don't even know Aunt Dominique! I'm going to stay here and take care of you." She had even stamped her foot for emphasis.

Her mother had tried to soothe her as best she could. "You are taking care of me, Brigitte, and that makes me very happy. But you will make me even happier, if I know you will be cared for after . . . "

"Don't say it!"

"Afterwards," Sandrine had said—gently—as she raised her hand from the bed's coverlet and waved two fingers in the air. Brigitte remembered thinking her mother's gesture was like shooing away a fly.

"I don't want to go to Paris, and I don't think Aunt Dominique really wants me to come live with her, either. She says she and Uncle Georges have spoken about 'the situation' as if I caused it—or you did. I'm old enough to stay here in Warsaw, Mama. I am. I can take care of myself."

"You are so like me, my dear," Sandrine sighed. "You act, and then you think. You need to think, and then act. You are fourteen, and you cannot be alone in Warsaw at fourteen."

Brigitte had tried again. "Mama, Aunt Dominique sounds mean." She picked up the crumpled ball of paper, opened it and read aloud, " 'Had you not gone off to Poland. . . .' She makes you sound like a criminal running away from the police. You came with Father."

Brigitte loved the story of how her parents met in Paris, how her French grandparents disapproved of the dashing young Pole who came courting their daughter, and how the couple eloped, then settled in Warsaw, where she had been born. True, an accident at the factory had claimed her father's life when she was six, but she still remembered him, and every detail of this story.

"Dominique means well," Sandrine had said in a tired voice. "She was the firstborn in the family, and I was the baby. She was always careful and thoughtful, while I was impetuous and headstrong—not unlike you, my dear," she had added with a small smile. Brigitte remembered how her mother had paused at this point, letting her eyes rest for a moment on the daughter who was so like her. "Your aunt wanted things to be just so, and I am not a 'just-so' girl. She thought marrying your father and moving to his country was an act of rebellion. I saw it as an act of love. Still, she has a good heart, Brigitte, and she will give you a home and a future."

Chapter 2

THE FAMILY

"ARE YOU BRIGITTE?" The voice was so like her mother's it startled her. A tall, thin woman was hurrying toward her, accompanied by a man who was much shorter and much fatter. Both stopped a foot away, as if they were unsure what should happen next.

Brigitte dropped a small curtsy, and the woman's face broke into a relieved smile.

"You are the image of Sandrine. I would know you anywhere. Look at that blond hair! Look at those freckles!" she demanded of no one in particular. "I am your Aunt Dominique. Welcome, Brigitte. Welcome to Paris." She gave Brigitte an awkward hug, and Brigitte noticed the smallest glitter of tears in her aunt's eyes as she stepped back.

"This is your uncle Georges," Dominique said, pulling her husband toward them by his sleeve.

The man bent over and kissed the top of Brigitte's hand. "*Enchanté*, my dear," he said.

Brigitte managed to stammer a "*bonjour*" in return before her aunt began talking again. "Your French is adequate," she said. "At least Sandrine taught you her mother's tongue."

Brigitte was tempted to add that she spoke Polish and a little Russian, too, but before the words bubbled out, Dominique nodded toward an attractive but rather severe-looking boy standing just behind Georges. "This is Henri Burtsev. He helps me at the café. You two will work together now."

Her aunt's letter had not mentioned anyone else, and Brigitte had spent the past three weeks thinking that there would be just three people at the Café Dominique—she, her aunt, and her uncle. The idea of someone to help her, someone closer to her own age, came as a surprise, and her heavy heart lifted just a bit. She studied the boy for a moment. Medium complexion, broad nose, black hair combed back from his forehead with no part. And his eyes: they were dark—and wary, she thought. He appeared to be older than she, though not by more than a few years, she guessed.

"*Bonjour*," Henri said, in an accent that, while not French, was vaguely familiar.

"Are you Polish?" Brigitte asked, spirits brightening.

"Russian," the boy answered.

"Russian? *Henri* isn't Russian."

"Brigitte, you must learn to curb your tongue. A refined young woman does not comment on a person's name." Dominique pursed her lips in disapproval and attempted to change the subject. "Henri has been with us for . . . how long would you say it has been, Henri?"

"Ten months, Madame," the boy answered. He looked at Brigitte and turned one corner of his mouth up in a small smile. "And no, Henri is not my real name."

Brigitte was intrigued. "Well, what is your real na—" she started to ask, when Dominique cut her off.

"He has told you. His name is Henri. He came to me as a kind of miracle. I needed help at the café, I put a sign in the window and—*voilà!*—within two days Henri appeared at my door. An answer to my prayers, I tell you."

"Or to the sign in the window," Georges said with a smile.

Dominique shook her head at her husband. "Do not be sacrilegious, Georges! Henri's father was a chef himself, and now Henri makes a *cassoulet* as well as I."

"No one makes a *cassoulet* as well as you, my dear," said Georges, looking at his wife fondly.

Dominique did not wait for a response, and in an

abrupt change of tone added, "Enough of this chit-chat. We must get home. There's work to do at the café."

⌦

"I hope you don't mind the open carriage," said Dominique after the horses began to pull away from the station. "Since it is such a lovely day and not too cold, I hired this one—to allow you to see something of Paris before we make our way to Montmartre. Would you like that?" Dominique was busily tucking a carriage robe over her knees and Brigitte's.

"Yes!" Brigitte answered, a bit surprised at the lift in her spirits. But then a twinge of guilt made her smile fade as quickly as it had bloomed.

The change in expression wasn't lost on Dominique, who quickly asked, "What is it, child?"

"Nothing."

"It is something," said Dominique. "I can tell."

Brigitte drew in a breath. Something about her aunt's question demanded an answer—of sorts. "I was just thinking . . . about my mother. She told me I would love Paris. She said it was full of excitement, adventure, and . . ."

"And what?" her aunt prodded gently.

"And I suppose I feel a little guilty about looking

forward to anything so soon after Mama's . . ." Brigitte still had a hard time saying the word "death," but Dominique made it unnecessary with her interruption.

"Nonsense," the older woman said firmly. "You were a fine daughter. Sandrine said as much many times in her letters to us. Didn't she, Georges?" Dominique looked to her rotund husband for confirmation, and he nodded in silent agreement. Turning back to Brigitte, she continued. "Brigitte, you must not confuse guilt with sadness. Of course you miss your mother, and sadness is to be expected. But you mustn't feel guilty because you look forward. Life is for the living. You will do well to remember that."

"Yes, Aunt," Brigitte replied, not certain she believed a word of what her aunt had said.

Dominique gave the carriage robe a final tug and said, "Well, then. Are you ready for the tour of your new home to begin?"

Brigitte swallowed the aching lump in her throat. Paris was not home, but it was new—and new things were always exciting, even if they were also frightening. She managed a small smile and answered, "I'm ready."

Chapter 3

THE TOUR

AS THE CARRIAGE moved away from the station and onto the busy street, Dominique gestured toward the distance. "You see that tower over there? We call it the Tour Eiffel. It was built fifteen years ago, to celebrate the 100th anniversary of the revolution."

Brigitte craned to get a better look at the skeletal structure that rose on the horizon. "What revolution?" she asked.

"Why, the French Revolution, of course," said Henri. "Surely you've heard of it in Poland?"

Brigitte had never much cared for history classes at Saint Stanislaus, but something she had memorized for an examination popped into her mind, just when she needed it. Smiling brightly, she said, "*Liberté, Égalité,*

Fraternité. The motto of the French Revolution. You must forgive my momentary lapse. I'm travel weary."

Dominique looked at her niece with pride. "Very good!"

"Liberty, equality, brotherhood," Henri repeated with fervor, saluting in the direction of the stunning tower. "A noble motto for a noble cause."

Dominique managed a small, disapproving *"tsk"* before commenting, "Henri, what shall we do with you and your causes. . . ."

Henri's expression darkened quickly—and noticeably. Dominique shook her head. "Ahhh, there you are again—allowing your feelings to be read on your face."

"You do not know my feelings, Madame," Henri said.

Brigitte squirmed uncomfortably and Georges quickly spoke up. "Revolutions are more than a mere 'cause,' my dear. They're meant to change the way people live their lives. They can evoke strong feelings."

"Well, they're often quite bloody." Dominique shook her head in distaste.

"And necessary," Henri muttered in a barely audible voice. Then, louder, he addressed himself to Brigitte and said, "The answer to your previous question is Adrik."

"Adrik? What question?" Brigitte was confused by this odd boy who sat facing her in the carriage.

"My Russian name. It means dark. I got tired of explaining it to Parisians, so I changed it." He watched Brigitte carefully, assessing her reaction. Though the corners of his mouth had turned up, Brigitte would never have described the expression on his lips as a smile.

Dominique tossed her head and exclaimed, "Well, to us you are Henri and ever shall be. For goodness' sake, gentlemen, I don't want to talk about darkness, or revolutions. We are celebrating today. I want to talk about the tower."

Georges smiled indulgently at his wife. "Do go on, my dear."

"Well, when it was first built, most Parisians—and I was among them, mind you—thought Monsieur Eiffel's tower was quite ugly, but it has grown on us. Some say it will become the symbol of Paris one day." Dominique gave a small laugh. "I can't say I agree with that."

The horses clopped on and the tower faded from view. Brigitte twisted in her seat, looking one way, then another. She shaded her eyes against the sun and almost stood up, eager to take in every sight. Paris was so different from Warsaw, where winter came early and stayed late. Here, at the end of September, people were outside. Vendors were selling winter fruits and vegetables, pots and pans, aprons and tablecloths, calling out their goods' superiority as they pushed their carts along the cobblestone streets.

"What is that, Aunt?" Brigitte asked, pointing to a complicated contraption a man struggled to move up the street. A tin tub, with three buckets hanging from its sides and steam escaping beneath its lid, was mounted on top of a boiler. The entire apparatus was attached to a large cart.

Dominique looked to see what had claimed Brigitte's attention. "Oh, he's selling hot baths."

At that moment, the vendor began to cry out. "Baths! The water is hot! Get your baths!" Someone opened a window and signaled to him.

"Now watch," said Dominique. The man took one of the buckets, filled it with boiling water from the tub, and carried the water into the building.

Dominique continued to explain. "These are poor flats. They have no way to heat large amounts of water. They probably do well to heat enough for a pot of tea! If they want a bath, they have to buy hot water from a street vendor. We are fortunate at the café. We have our own well, and we can boil all the water we need. We bathe once a week. I insist on cleanliness."

The carriage had come to the bottom of a steep hill and was having difficulty making its way through the foot traffic. The driver slowed almost to a stop in front of a fairground dominated by a large pink tent. A wooden sign proclaimed "Cirque Medrano" in bold gilded letters. Posters of clowns, acrobats, bearded ladies, lions, and elephants were tacked onto poles around the entrance to the tent, which stood in the center of a small makeshift village. Smaller tents and cobbled-together shelters spread out across the field, and people huddled around charcoal fires, cooking and chatting. Babies toddled from one gathering to another, welcomed as if they were part of a larger family.

"Oh, look! A circus! My mother loved circuses! Have you ever been to this one?" Brigitte half-stood to get a better look, addressing her question to anyone in the carriage.

Dominique and Georges shook their heads. "We are far too busy at the café for an entertainment like this," Dominique said, flicking her hand toward the fairgrounds dismissively.

Disappointed, Brigitte looked at Henri. "Have you been to the circus, Henri?"

"Occasionally," the boy answered, staring absently into the crowd.

Not far away, an older man began to turn the crank of a barrel organ, and lively music spilled into the air. A monkey danced on the end of a leash, darting among the crowd, holding up a tin cup begging for coins.

"Look at the monkey!" Brigitte exclaimed. "Here, monkey!" The words were out of her mouth before she could think.

The organ grinder heard Brigitte's exclamation,

and with a flick of the leash, he encouraged the creature to jump into the carriage. Brigitte sat down promptly, and the monkey perched on her shoulders and began to examine her braid, holding it between two tiny paws. Then it peered into her face.

"Ohhhh," she exclaimed. "How darling!"

"Don't be flattered," said Henri. "He's looking for lice. Monkeys do that."

"You won't find a snack there," Brigitte told the creature, as she tried to tug her braid out of its brown paws.

"Lice! Get that dirty little beast out of here!" Dominique exclaimed, shrinking back into her seat as far as she could go.

"But Aunt Dominique," Brigitte said, "I have no lice. . . ."

Brigitte was saved from further discussion of lice by a boy who suddenly leaned into the carriage and called, "*Aqui*, Toulouse!" At the sound of his voice, the monkey leapt from Brigitte's shoulders toward the boy, who was dressed in the strange, tight clothing of an acrobat—Brigitte had to think of the French word—a *saltimbanque*.

"I am so sorry, Mademoiselle, Madame," he said as he bent to retrieve the loose end of the leash. Brigitte strained to understand. The boy's French was heavily accented with Spanish.

"Toulouse responds to me best if I speak to him in Spanish. But for you . . . I shall practice my French."

He nodded toward Brigitte and Dominique before retrieving the end of the monkey's leash which was dragging on the ground. When he looked up, his eyes fell on Henri.

"Monsieur," he said, nodding his head in greeting. Henri gave a dismissive nod in return, and the *saltimbanque* looked at Georges. "Toulouse can have a mind of his own, but he means no harm. I apologize for a creature who cannot speak for itself. I shall take him back to Romero."

As quickly as they had appeared, the boy and the monkey retreated toward the man with the barrel organ, who immediately began to crank up a tune. Soon the monkey was dancing among the crowd, begging for change. At each *ping* of a coin dropping into his cup, Toulouse rewarded the donor with a tip of his tiny cap and a yellow-toothed smile.

Henri watched, shaking his head. "People are starving, and the bourgeoisie pay money to see a monkey smile. It makes little sense to me."

"What's bourgeois?" Brigitte asked.

"You're bourgeois," Henri answered with a half-smile.

"I am not!" Brigitte protested, not knowing what the word meant but disliking the sound of it.

"But of course you are bourgeois, child, and you should take pride in the fact. It is an accomplishment to be part of the middle class and have a trade."

"Then may I have a coin for the monkey, Aunt?" said Brigitte hopefully.

"Certainly not," Dominique answered quickly. "Henri seems to think the bourgeoisie do not know the value of a franc, but I assure you this one does."

"I know how you value a coin, Madame," Henri said smoothly, then quickly changed the subject. "He's a clever one, that Romero. If he weren't a gypsy, he'd be bourgeoisie himself. He's already got the monkey working for him. For peanuts."

"That's a good one, Henri," Georges said, chuckling. "For peanuts."

Henri did not favor Georges with a smile, and Brigitte felt a wave of irritation and disappointment rise in her. Why couldn't he smile at Georges's small joke? "Who is Romero?" she asked, eager to break the awkward silence. "Is he the *saltimbanque?*"

Henri shook his head. "Romero's the one who owns the monkey."

"And the *saltimbanque* . . ." Before she could get her question out, Brigitte saw him in the crowd and stood to get a better view. "Look, Aunt! There he is! He's walking on his hands!"

"Brigitte! Sit down, please, and remember: young ladies do not raise their voices, and they most certainly do not point." Dominique looked shocked, but Brigitte saw her aunt pull a pair of glasses out of her purse, snap open their handle, and hold them up to her eyes to get a better look.

"That boy—I thought he looked familiar. Haven't I seen him before?" she asked Henri. "I must confess to closing my eyes when that little beast was in the carriage."

"You have, Madame," said Henri. "He's Paco de Suarez. He comes to the café occasionally to meet Picasso. He's modeling for him these days. That's his younger sister, Anna Maria. She poses for Picasso, too." Henri gestured toward a young girl in a pink and black ballet costume, who was expertly turning somersaults on the back of an enormous white horse. Brigitte watched, entranced, willing the crowd to continue its press against the carriage, and force it to stay still a moment or so longer.

Dominique studied the *saltimbanque* and his sister more closely. "Yes, that's right," she said slowly. "I've never seen the girl, but he comes to the café. However, he never eats." She shook her head.

"Well, he has no money, just like the rest of them," said Henri, making a sweeping gesture that took in all the street performers, who were busily standing on balancing balls, juggling, and doing anything else it took to entice the crowd inside the tent.

Dominique sniffed. "Perhaps they have no money because they have no ambition."

"They look as if they are working hard to me,"

Brigitte said quickly. "And people are paying admissions. Where does that money go?"

"In the manager's pocket," Henri answered with disgust.

"Well, they must pay the performers something. . . ." Brigitte protested.

Georges leaned forward and awkwardly patted the carriage robe near Brigitte's knee. "Do not worry, my dear. I'm certain the performers are paid a wage of some kind. And as for the manager's pockets . . ." The older man turned toward Henri. "Why, even our young friend here must admit managers are worthy of a wage, as well. After all, it is the managers who hire the performers and thereby create the circus. It's simple. No circus, no jobs."

"I stand corrected, Monsieur," Henri said coolly. "I humbly apologize. Indeed, it is the managers who hire and fire."

Brigitte stole a glance at Henri. He didn't seem humble—or apologetic—to her.

"Now, don't get touchy, my boy. There's no need for apology," Georges said good-naturedly. "I'd say these performers are among the lucky ones. The Medrano is the most exciting circus in Paris, and its acts are among the most exciting—and daring—in the city." Georges was thoughtful for a moment before adding, "Though of course, people do get hurt."

Dominique sniffed. "Not to worry. It's the life they choose."

Georges added, "Correct, my dear. Indeed, I would add it is the life they are born to. Wandering gypsies—that's what they are."

Wandering gypsies.

Brigitte loved the sound of those words, and she turned them over in her head. Wandering gypsies. "I'd love to see them perform," she said, then quickly added, "but I wouldn't want to see anyone get hurt."

Dominique pursed her lips as if the conversation had suddenly turned distasteful. "You have much to learn at the café, Brigitte. The circus will have to wait."

As the crowds began to move inside, the carriage slowly rolled forward. Brigitte caught a final glimpse of Paco de Suarez, walking on two hands as easily as most people use two feet. Despite the fact that it was housed in a tent, the Cirque Medrano looked as if it were permanently anchored to its spot at the bottom of the butte of Montmartre. It wasn't going anywhere, and as the bright pink tent dropped from view, and the cobblestone streets of Paris gave way to the dirt roads and steep slopes of Montmartre, Brigitte told herself she could wait. The monkey and the *saltimbanque* would be there, and she intended to see them both again.

Chapter 4
THE CAFÉ

"**NOW WE ARE COMING** to Montmartre, home of the Café Dominique."

Brigitte noticed the pride in her aunt's voice at the mention of the café, and said, "I'm eager to see it, Aunt. Mother often said your café must be just like the Zlota."

Dominique sniffed. "I don't know your Zlota, my dear, but I can assure you the Café Dominique is not 'just like' any other café in the world."

Brigitte squirmed uncomfortably. She had insulted her aunt, when she only meant a compliment. Before she became ill, Brigitte's mother had loved to walk with her around Warsaw, often passing by the elegant Café Zlota. Brigitte loved to peer through the lace-curtained windows. Each table had fresh flowers in small crystal vases. Well-dressed customers laughed and chatted together as if they had not a care in the world, while a gypsy walked among the customers, playing on his violin. Once, her mother had surprised Brigitte by steering her inside, where they took a small table near the back of the room. They had ordered tea, and it was served from china cups so thin they were almost transparent. Somehow tea sipped from these cups tasted far better than tea sipped from the thick brown mugs at home. Hadn't Dominique just said her café was much better than the Zlota? Brigitte felt a rush of anticipation.

Dominique's voice interrupted Brigitte's train of thought as the carriage moved up the hill. "We have excellent wineries here, and even our own mills to grind the flour for the café. Now, of course, the artists and the writers are taking over. The bohemians." She sniffed, and Georges *tsk*ed supportively.

"Bohemians?" Brigitte asked.

"Free spirits," Dominique said quickly. "They think their own thoughts, write their own opinions, paint their own art—without any regard for the constraints of normal society. They are a breed apart, and sadly, many of them come to my café."

Brigitte's interest quickened. She had never seen a bohemian and couldn't wait to do so.

Eventually the carriage came to a small square and

drew up to a narrow, three-story building with the words "Café Dominique" painted prominently over the entranceway. Georges paid the driver, and the party waited while Dominique fumbled inside her purse and found a large brass key.

A sign that said "*Fermé*" hung on the door, and Dominique, who never closed her café except on Christmas Day, flipped it over to read "*Ouvert.*" Then she unlocked the heavy door and pushed it open.

"*Voilà,*" she said with a flourish, as if she were welcoming Brigitte to the Palace of Versailles.

Brigitte stepped inside, and her heart sank. Indeed, the Café Dominique was not "just like" the Zlota. The low ceiling gave the small room an oppressive feel, and the dark wood walls closed it in further. Rough wooden tables, some with benches and others with chairs, filled the space. Brigitte noticed the tabletops were pockmarked with initials and other graffiti, and thoughts of her mother saying Dominique liked things "just so" came rushing back to her. How could her aunt tolerate her furniture being defaced by rowdy customers?

"I see you're looking at the tabletops," Dominique said, following Brigitte's gaze around the room. "There's little point in sanding them down. Those bohemians will just carve their initials again. What can I say? A fool's name is often seen in a public place."

Suddenly Brigitte felt heavy inside. Whether it was from travel weariness, disappointment in the café, or both, she could not have said. She was grateful when Dominique said, "We'll show you to your room now. Follow me." As she followed her aunt toward a narrow staircase that led off the kitchen, Brigitte wondered if there would be time for a brief nap on a real bed. The seat on the train had been so uncomfortable that sheer exhaustion forced the catnap she took before the train pulled into Paris. Had that been only a few short hours ago?

Dominique began climbing the stairs and issuing orders. "Georges, bring Brigitte's bags, please. Henri, you'd best get a start on the dinner preparations. I will need you to bring fifteen kilos of potatoes from the cellar. We were not open for lunch, and I cannot miss dinner."

Georges was huffing by the time he had finished carrying Brigitte's bags up the two flights of stairs that led to her attic room. He straightened up, and with difficulty said, "Welcome, my dear—huh, to your—huh—to your new home."

Suddenly Brigitte thought of her father. Since he had died when she was a small child, she had only vague memories of him, but they were good ones. She managed a tired smile for her uncle, another kind man, and looked around her new bedroom.

A narrow iron bed was pushed up under a slanting eave. It seemed to have a fresh coat of white paint, and it was covered with a patchwork quilt of blue and yellow calico squares. Brigitte glanced at the bed with longing, but some instinct told her not to sit down. Not yet. A rather pretty armoire stood opposite the bed, and next to it, there was a simple table with a pitcher and wash-basin on top. A rag rug and a straight-back chair finished off the room's furnishings. *Well,* Brigitte thought, *Aunt Dominique said it was small and comfortable, and tucked this far up in the attic, it has to be safe.*

Dominique was opening the casement window. "Come, Brigitte. Look. From your window you can see the domes of Sacré Coeur at the top of the hill. The hill's martyrs are buried in its crypts."

Brigitte walked over to peer out. The three white, onion-shaped domes of the cathedral gleamed in the afternoon sun. It was beautiful, but Brigitte didn't want to think about crypts. She looked away, down to the square below.

A young man, dressed in the typical workingman's black cap and blue jacket, stood surrounded by a small group of children. He was short—no taller than five feet, she guessed—and muscular, like an athlete. He had a head full of thick black hair, and a few locks dipped down over his left eye. But it was his hands that captured Brigitte's attention. They were small and delicate—almost like a girl's hand, she thought to herself. The man was using a long stick to draw figures in the dirt of the square, to the delight of a few children who were watching him. Fascinated, Brigitte watched, too. He drew with one long, continuous stroke, never hesitating, never lifting the stick from the ground. First, a rabbit, then a dog took shape in the sand. The images were unmistakable, even from a third-floor window. A few of the children had sticks of their own and were trying to copy what the young man was doing.

Dominique joined Brigitte at the window and followed her gaze. "That's the painter we talked about earlier."

Brigitte was confused. "Painter?" she said.

"Yes, yes," Dominique said, "the Spaniard. His name is Pablo Picasso. He often draws like that for the neighborhood children."

"Oh . . . is he the one the *saltimbanque* poses for?"

Dominique nodded. "Well, many people pose for him but yes, the *saltimbanque* from this afternoon—he is one of Picasso's models." Dominique watched the activity for a moment more, then looked at Brigitte.

"Unpack your things and don't waste time watching him. Now that the café is open, he'll be downstairs soon enough, ruining my napkins with his incessant sketches. Why he brings no proper paper is beyond my comprehension."

Dominique shook her head at the reminder of the extra work it took to scrub Picasso's quick sketches out of her napkins. "Come along, Georges. Brigitte, find Henri when you come down. He will need help peeling those potatoes."

Brigitte put her things away quickly and turned the covers back on her bed so it would be ready to welcome her as soon as she could decently say goodnight. Then she hurried down to the kitchen. It was time to go to work.

Chapter 5

THE KNIFE

WITHIN A MONTH of her arrival, any excitement or anticipation that Brigitte felt as she contemplated her future had given way to a depression that weighed her down like a woolen cape soaked by a rainstorm. Her mother had said she would love Paris, but she missed Poland. Her mother had said the café would be full of excitement, but she found it full of hard work. She made countless trips to the well for water and to the root cellar for vegetables, and the muscles in her back, arms, and legs ached from the new stress. She chopped kindling for the fire, singeing her fingers as she tried to build the flames—or damp them down. On a rare occasion when her aunt sent her on an errand that took her reasonably close, Brigitte had managed to pass by the Medrano, hoping to catch another glimpse of the sidewalk show—and the *saltimbanque*. She often remembered Henri's words, spoken on her first day in Paris. "He's Paco de Suarez. He comes to the café occasionally to meet Picasso." Although she watched for him daily, Brigitte had not seen the *saltimbanque* at the café. Not even once.

On the other hand—true to Dominique's prediction—Picasso was there every day, along with his friends. They seemed to move together as one, and had even given themselves a name—*bande à Picasso*. They laughed uproariously, talked about art, argued about politics, and drank altogether too much. Despite the heat of their arguments, Brigitte had noticed that they arrived as friends, and left as friends, no matter how heated their discussions had become. Once she heard Picasso's mistress—the woman they called Fernande—say, "I'd like to wave a banner that says, 'Make way for artists, the only people with the right to live outside society.' "

Although her aunt took a dim view of them, Brigitte wondered what it would be like to be a bohemian or a *saltimbanque*. What would it feel like to say what you think and do what you want, without giving a fig about Aunt Dominique's "society" and what it thought was proper? *Before long, when I take care of myself, I'll find out*, Brigitte told herself as she reached

into the wicker basket that held the never-ending supply of clean napkins that needed folding.

Nearby, Henri was preparing to turn a large leg of
lamb into the neat cubes of meat that went into
Dominique's famous *cassoulet*. In the short while she
had been at the café, Brigitte had learned that, for
Henri, food was as much about performance as it was
preparation. Despite her gloomy mood, she watched
as the boy carefully surveyed Dominique's kitchen
knives. He selected the carving knife with the slim
bone handle—the prize of her aunt's vast collection.
Henri raised the knife like a conductor raising a baton,
and then came the downbeat—a swift pass through
the carcass, and a neat slice of meat fell away. Then
a series of staccato *thwack, thwack, thwack*s, and the
lamb was rendered into small cubes, which he deftly
scraped into a waiting pottery bowl, and the process
began again.

Brigitte watched, fascinated. Then when she could
bear it no longer, she jumped from her stool. "Let me
try, Henri," she said, reaching for the knife. "Folding
napkins is boring."

Henri paused in mid-*thwack* and looked at her in
surprise. "Don't be a goose. I am a chef. This is my job.
Yours is to wait on the tables."

"Well, I'm supposed to learn how to cook. Aunt
Dominique has said so, and you're supposed to teach

me. Now let me try!" said Brigitte, grabbing the knife from Henri's grasp.

The sharp blade cut cleanly, and at first, Brigitte felt no pain. Then she saw the blood running down her wrist.

"I've cut my wrist! I could die!" Her hand was throbbing now, and she thought of every book she had read or tale she had heard where the heroine dies from slashing a wrist.

Henri grabbed a napkin from the stack and dabbed at the wound until he could see it clearly. "You've cut your palm, not your wrist. It's not even deep. Here, keep the napkin pressed against it," he said as he bent to retrieve the knife from the stone floor, holding it up to inspect its edge. "Good. The blade isn't damaged." He looked at Brigitte. "And you will survive. Children shouldn't play with knives," he added, before returning to his task.

"I am not a child!" Brigitte exclaimed, angry tears threatening to spill. "I can take care of myself—and I soon will. I—I hate this café! I told Mama I would hate it, and I do. It's boring, and hard and—and I
. . . " Brigitte's hand was throbbing, but she noticed that the red stain was no longer spreading, so she let her statement trail off. She wasn't sure how it was going to end, anyway.

"How odd life is," Henri said as he continued to

chop. "The café is yours, and you hate it; it could never be mine . . ." There was a pause, more chops with the knife, and then he added softly, ". . . and I . . . well, for a bourgeoisie pursuit, it is rather nice."

"Well, I suspect that Aunt Dominique will cling to this café for years to come," Brigitte said. "But you could have one like it. Maybe back in Russia some day."

Henri laughed and shook his head. "I could never have anything back in Russia. Not a flat of my own—and certainly not a café."

"Why not?" Brigitte asked innocently. "If you work hard and save your money—"

Henri laughed unpleasantly. "Spoken like a naive child. No one has anything in Russia. The tsars have it all—the land, the money, the power. But . . ." Henri's mood seemed to brighten for a moment. "Things are changing in my homeland. One day, the wealth will be redistributed and shared. As Karl Marx once said, 'From each according to his ability; to each according to his need.' "

"How would that happen?" Brigitte asked. "Everyone doesn't have equal abilities—or equal needs."

Henri's eyebrows rose, and his mouth twisted into a slight smile. "You'll see," he said.

"Well, as for me, I can't imagine why anyone would want a café in the first place—here, or in Russia. Serfs don't work as hard as I do. Plus the patrons! They ask for one thing, change their mind, then ask for another. Then they argue with me when I serve them. I try to tell them it's what they ordered, and they say it's not what they had in mind. Sometimes I want to pour a pitcher of water over them!"

"Brigitte!"

Brigitte jumped at the sound of her aunt's voice. Dominique stood in the back doorway, the day's produce in the basket she carried. Georges stood in her shadow, a wrapped wheel of sharp cheese clutched under his arm.

"I can only hope my ears deceived me," Dominique said, handing Georges her basket. "You must not *think* of pouring pitchers of water on customers."

"I wasn't serious, Aunt," Brigitte said, making a mental note that she must confess this lie to the priest at Sacré Coeur before Mass on Sunday.

Chapter 6

THE REQUEST

I'VE TOLD YOU, we have an odd mix here at the café," Dominique explained as she hung her cloak on a peg by the door. "True, some are demanding and rude, but there are the others as well. Monsieur Pavlov, for example, is a gentleman and a diplomat." Dominique's face broke into a smile at the mention of the café's most regular paying customer, but it faded quickly when she noticed the blood-stained napkin. The color drained from the older woman's face. "Goodness! What has happened here?" she demanded.

"It's nothing, Aunt. I was . . . clumsy with the knife." Brigitte quickly looked to Henri to see if he would say more, but he was concentrating on cubes of lamb and didn't look up.

"Let me see," Dominique said, gently lifting the napkin to inspect the wound. "*Tsk*. It is nothing—as you say—and will heal nicely. Cuts and cooks go together, though you should learn to be more careful." She shook out the napkin and studied it. "I believe this one is for the rag bin now. Blood is a difficult stain to remove, and I see there are still traces of Picasso's sketches on it." Dominique sighed in frustration as she tossed the napkin into the box that held rags waiting to be washed. She turned and addressed Brigitte once again.

"Speaking of our customers, I have made a decision. Henri, I need your attention as well."

The steady thwacking sound stopped, and two sets of young eyes focused on Dominique. "I have decided that Brigitte should be making the Friday deliveries to Monsieur Pavlov's office."

"But, Madame!" Henri protested. "That has been my job! And, and—and after all, he is my countryman."

"Yes, so you've said. But you are from the Georgia region, isn't that correct? Pavlov is from St. Petersburg."

"Hardly neighbors, my boy," Georges said with a small smile in Henri's direction. "Russia is a vast empire."

Dominique tied an apron on and continued to talk. "Brigitte has served Pavlov well here in the café; he has told me so himself."

"But I speak to him in his native tongue!"

"Well, I greet him with *privyet* and say *do svidaniya* when he leaves," Brigitte said.

"Yes, I have heard you," Dominique said approvingly. She peered closely at Henri, who looked as if someone had landed a fist in his stomach. "This is Pavlov's request." Dominique said gently. "I've been meaning to ask. Have you done something that would offend him?"

"Why do you assume ill of me?" Henri said angrily. "I haven't done a thing to that . . . to Pavlov, other than say, 'Good evening,' 'Good night,' and 'Do you prefer the red wine, or the white?' "

Brigitte noticed that Henri's hand—the one that still held the knife—was white-knuckled and shaking.

"Now, now, my boy. No one assumes ill of you," Georges said soothingly. "It's just that Pavlov . . . well, he is a good customer, and we like to please the good ones."

"Yes," Dominique quickly agreed. "Unlike those anarchists who try my patience. . . ."

Brigitte knew about bohemians, but anarchists? She looked at her Uncle Georges. "What's an anarchist?" she asked.

"What's an anarchist?" Henri rolled his eyes to the ceiling of the room. "You have more questions than a schoolteacher. An anarchist is not a 'what.' It's a 'who.' An anarchist is . . ."

Brigitte's voice trembled with sudden anger. She was weary of this boy who was not as helpful as she had hoped. "I wasn't asking you, Henri. I was asking my uncle."

"There, there, both of you," Georges said. He folded the paper he had started to read and walked over to Brigitte, putting his arm around her shoulder. "Anarchism is a . . . a different way of thinking, my dear. Anarchists seem to want freedom without any limits." Georges shook his head. "Of course that doesn't work."

"Well, if freedom has limits on it, then it's not really freedom. . . ." Brigitte began to say, until Dominique stopped her with an upheld hand.

"Anarchists want to overthrow the government!" the older woman whispered dramatically, looking around the kitchen as if one were hiding in the pantry.

"I thought that had already happened here in France," Brigitte said, confused. "There was the revolution. . . ."

"Well, my dear, revolutions tend to be contagious," Uncle Georges said. "Unrest has spread across Europe—even into your homeland," Georges said, addressing Henri.

"And high time it has," Henri replied, as he continued to render the lamb into neat little cubes.

"Well, it is one thing for Russia to be in turmoil;

another for it to spread to France." Georges let out his breath in a sigh. "Montmartre is turning into something of a hotbed, and the gendarmes seem to take . . . ," he paused, ". . . a special interest in some of our regular customers. I think they may suspect some of them."

"Which ones? Of what?" Brigitte asked, more than a little intrigued. She considered the customers who came to the café. How could she have missed a genuine anarchist?

"Ah, well, I hate to say so, but Picasso, and his friend Guillaume Apollinaire, and some of the others, too, appear to have garnered some suspicion," said Georges uncomfortably. "I'm sure it is nothing, I'm sure they are quite respectable, as artists and poets go. Today our police seem to be eager to find anarchy lurking behind every casual conversation."

Brigitte looked directly at Henri, but he avoided her gaze.

Dominique sniffed. "Enough of politics, Georges. I thought you were talking about our customers. I scarcely consider Picasso and Apollinaire to be customers. They live from hand to mouth, with everything on credit. And every so often a painting in payment! That's not a customer to me. Really, Georges, you are too good to them! Now Monsieur Pavlov—*there* is a valued customer, dining with us practically every day, and paying for his meals with good French francs. You are to be certain his Friday meal arrives on time and in good condition, Brigitte. Do you understand? As a reward, you may take a few hours on Friday afternoons for yourself."

The prospect of a few hours of freedom renewed Brigitte's spirit. "Oh, I'll take very good care of Monsieur Pavlov, Aunt. I promise." *And then*, she thought, . . . *and then, I'll do as I please with the time I have left.*

Chapter 7

THE PATRONS

THE FOLLOWING EVENING, Brigitte was alone in the kitchen, hard at work popping peas from their pods. It was a sitting-down job, and Brigitte—grateful for the respite—was beginning to allow her mind to wander into a pleasant daydream when Henri walked into the kitchen.

"Put those down," he said importantly. "Come help me wait the tables. Picasso and his friends are here. They've ordered the *cassoulet*."

Without looking up from her task, Brigitte said, "Is there no word for 'please' in Russian? In French, it's *s'il vous plaît*. You might try that."

Henri made no response and busied himself putting the *cassoulet* on a large serving tray, while

Brigitte—sighing heavily to show her displeasure at his rudeness—put the bowl of peas on the counter and reached for a stack of white plates. She began counting them out. "Let me see . . . Apollinaire, Fernande, Max Jacob, Picasso—that's four," she said aloud, happy to show off that she had learned the names of Picasso's friends.

"It's five now," Henri said, glancing into the dining room. "The *saltimbanque* is here. No doubt he'll want to be fed, too."

Brigitte's scalp tingled. She reached to smooth her braid, afraid the kind of electricity she felt had made it frizz. Paco de Suarez. At last.

In a tone she hoped sounded as casual as if she were asking Henri to pass the salt, she said, "The boy from the circus? The one with the monkey?"

"Yes, the boy from the circus," Henri said, smirking and mimicking her tone. Then he added, "Your face turns red, like a cabbage."

Voices raised in argument stopped their conversation, and Henri walked toward the doorway. "Shhhh," he cautioned, holding a hand up for silence. "Your *saltimbanque* and Picasso are arguing."

"Ohhh . . . he's not my *saltimbanque*, Henri!" Brigitte insisted, even as she slipped beside Henri and shamelessly joined him in eavesdropping. She recognized Picasso's voice, rising in irritation, and another

47

anxious voice—it had to be Paco's—trying to explain. One did not need to speak Spanish to understand that much.

Fernande's voice interrupted the argument. "Oh, my love. Have a little mercy. The boy is merely late. A model's life is hard. I should know that, shouldn't I?"

Brigitte listened, remembering other outbursts from the temperamental young artist. To herself she said, *I don't care if he draws for small children in the square— Picasso is really quite rude.*

There was another exclamation from Picasso, and Fernande once again replied in simple, uncomplicated French, her tone soothing and gentle. "We are having a fine meal, and it's not yet midnight. You still have the whole night ahead of you to paint. But first let us eat. I'm starving, and I'm certain everyone else is, too."

With that comment, Henri hurried through the door with Brigitte close on his heels. Henri stopped right in front of Fernande. "It's so good to see you again, Madame, and the rest of the—what is that clever name you call yourselves?" he asked, as he placed the large platter in the center of the table.

"*Le bande à Picasso,*" Fernande answered gaily.

"Well, you must not let this band of men keep you away for so long. You have not been dining at the Lapin Agile, have you?"

Everyone at the table burst into laughter—except

Picasso, who now stared out the window into the darkness of the square. Henri was undaunted and continued his banter. "Max," he said, touching the shoulder of a small balding man wearing a monocle. "How goes the writing?"

Max Jacob shifted his attention from the others and looked up at Henri, giving him a courteous, but somewhat dismissive, nod.

Brigitte stood transfixed, the heavy weight of the tray, with its jug of wine, glasses, and empty plates forgotten. Was this surly Henri—joking with the customers, talking about a rival café? She stole a glance at Paco, who stood silently in his skintight costume, waiting for a signal from the artist. He caught Brigitte's glance and smiled. Actually smiled! Brigitte almost dropped her tray.

Henri snapped his fingers at Brigitte. "Plates, please."

Brigitte's mouth formed an O, and she stifled angry words. Who was Henri to use that imperious tone with her? How dare he treat her like a scullery maid! Hot words bubbled to her lips, but before she could say anything to put Henri in his place, the *saltimbanque* was at her side.

"Allow me, Mademoiselle," Paco said in Spanish-accented French. "This tray must be heavy."

"I can do it," Brigitte protested.

"Of course you can," he said, taking the tray from her arms. "But so can I." Paco deftly placed a plate in front of each of the diners, and handed the now-empty tray back to Brigitte. He did not take a seat, but remained standing, looking directly at her. "I remember you from the carriage—in front of the circus."

Brigitte felt a blush creep up her cheek. He remembered her!

"And I have seen you occasionally, when you have come by the Medrano in the afternoons—to watch Toulouse."

Without thinking, Brigitte let her mouth fall open. She never thought anyone had paid the slightest attention to her in that crowd. And though she had not been forbidden to go Brigitte felt certain, without knowing exactly why, her aunt would not approve of these little detours to the circus on her way back to the café.

Before she could say another word, Brigitte felt, rather than saw, two eyes staring at her. She didn't need to look in order to know it was the now-familiar stare of the painter. Brigitte had served Picasso and his party several times since she had come to the café, yet she still was not used to the intensity of his gaze. His eyes glittered, reminding her of two black marbles shining in the sun. She stared back at Picasso, knowing it was rude, yet unable to help herself. Slowly, the painter smiled at her, and Brigitte could not resist smiling back. It happened every time she saw him.

Fernande watched the exchange carefully. "Now then," she said briskly. "Here is our food. Let us enjoy." She lifted a glass of wine. "*Bon appétit!*"

Picasso hooked an extra chair with his foot, pulling it over to the table and patting its seat as he gestured to Paco. It was an invitation to eat, and Brigitte took note of how quickly Paco sat down. Exhaustion—and eagerness—made her wish she could do the same.

Chapter 8

LE BANDE À PICASSO

HENRI HAD TAKEN OVER serving Picasso's party, and Brigitte busied herself darting from table to table, trying to satisfy everyone's demands, which seemed to grow louder and more insistent with each glass of wine. Despite her best intentions, she could not keep herself from moving as close to Picasso's table as she could. Paco was wolfing down the *cassoulet* as if he hadn't eaten in days, and when he caught her glance, he smiled. Tired as she was, Brigitte managed a small smile in return, and in an effort to stay nearby—and since Henri had disappeared to bring another pitcher of wine—she began to wipe up spills that were creeping across the tabletop and listen in to the stories that were being told.

Picasso's friend Apollinaire was talking. When he spoke, his voice had the modulated tones of a professional orator, rich and deep. He postured as if he were used to having people hang on his every word. Brigitte was working on a stubborn bit of cheese stuck to the tabletop and stole glances at the huge man. *Well, he may be a poet,* she thought, *but his head is shaped like a pear!*

"Pablo," Apollinaire said, "I've been thinking about the painting you are working on—the large one for which our young *saltimbanque* friend here poses." Apollinaire paused and pulled a slim magazine from his coat pocket. "As I say in my review of your earlier circus paintings, 'One feels that his slender acrobats, glowing in their rags, are true sons of the people: versatile, cunning, dexterous, poverty-stricken, and lying.' "

Picasso nodded his agreement, and Brigitte was shocked. How could Apollinaire talk this way—and Picasso agree with him—right in front of Paco? They had called him a liar! She continued to wipe the clean tabletop and stole glances at Paco, wondering how he would respond. Wouldn't he be insulted? To her surprise, he didn't seem to be the least bothered by the remarks. In fact, a small smile played around his mouth. *Why, he agrees with Apollinaire,* Brigitte thought in amazement.

Apollinaire saw Brigitte's look of surprise and smiled at her, including her in his audience.

"Don't look so shocked, my dear. I mean no insult, and Paco knows that. All artists—writers, painters, and we include circus performers in this illustrious group—

are at odds with society. And so we should be. It's our job to show society for what it is—how it exploits the powerless. Our friend Picasso does just that with his art. The one he creates now will be a masterpiece."

"Well, I just hope the masterpiece is completed soon," Fernande said. "How many times can one paint a simple circus scene? Pablo has done it over many times, changing the background, adding characters, taking some away, seeking perfection. And when I think of the cost of the paint . . . and that huge canvas . . ." Fernande took a long sip on her wine. Brigitte wondered if she had spoken in fluid French to keep Picasso from easily following what she said. Was she complaining about him? Or commiserating with him?

As if in answer to Brigitte's unspoken question, Fernande blew a kiss at Picasso. "Pablo and I don't need society; only each other. I remember when we first met. In the evenings, I used to sit in front of my door on the Rue Ravignan and relax with a book until the sun set. By coincidence, Pablo lived there, too, in the same street, in the same building. I often saw him out in the square, talking nosily with his friends from Spain. I found them slightly—what shall I say? Annoying?" The little group burst into gales of laughter. "But colorful! They were very colorful!"

Brigitte dropped all pretext of working and simply stood, listening to this tale of how the lovers met.

Occasionally she let her eyes drift over to the *saltim-banque*, but he was concentrating on his meal.

"There was such a thunderstorm that day! The sky was black, and when the clouds suddenly broke I had to rush for shelter. You had a kitten in your arms, Pablo. Do you remember?"

Picasso was trying to light his pipe, and nodded agreement, so Fernande turned her attention back to the table. "Well, he tried to prevent me from passing. He kept offering me that kitten. I spoke French. He spoke Spanish—and a little broken French—but we both laughed, and the next thing you know, he took me to see his studio. . . ."

Fernande left the rest of the sentence to the imagination of her listeners, and Brigitte, aware that her cheeks were burning, avoided looking at anyone, as Fernande continued her tale. "Once I was in his studio, it became instantly obvious that here was an artist who worked hard and created many pieces, but *merci*, what a mess! There were canvases of all sizes scattered about, tubes of paint, paint brushes, turpentine, etching acid, pieces of sculpture—all necessary, but not all neat."

"Well, nothing has changed," said Apollinaire, and everyone at the table burst into laughter.

"Apollinaire!" cried Fernande in mock indignation. "Well, it has taken us some time to come to—how shall I say it—compatibility. But all is well now."

Max Jacob removed his monocle and polished it with his handkerchief. "I had forgotten you lived in the Bateau-Lavoir before Picasso moved in there," he said casually.

"Such a name you give our old ramshackle building, Max! A wash boat! But I must say it is apt. Our poor old Bateau-Lavoir does look like the boats on the Seine where the laundresses do their wash—does it not?"

Fernande ended her tale with a laugh and put her hand on Max Jacob's arm in a light gesture. Picasso's genial mood turned dark immediately. He scowled at Fernande, and as quickly as if Jacob's sleeve had caught fire, she removed her hand. An awkward silence settled around the table.

Picasso abruptly stood and looked at Paco. He crooked a finger in the boy's direction, and Paco—leaving his last bite of *cassoulet* on the plate—immediately rose to his feet, as did everyone else at the table.

Brigitte watched the now-subdued band of friends walk out into the dark Montmartre night. *Go. Work on your "masterpiece,"* she thought, marveling at the influence the small Spaniard wielded over those around him.

From a table not far away, Monsieur Pavlov raised a hand to Brigitte. As she approached, he put away the small notebook he was writing in, and asked for the check.

Chapter 9

THE CONVERSATION

ON SUNDAYS, the café did not open its doors until 2:00 P.M. Dominique reserved Sunday mornings for early Mass at Sacré Coeur and time in the kitchen to take stock of her larder and organize supplies for the coming week.

"Once these potatoes are peeled, Aunt, we will have only a few kilos left," Brigitte said, eyeing a mound of dusty brown russets in a basket by the stove.

Dominique nodded and added *pommes de terre* to her shopping list. "That reminds me—you and Henri should scrub the potatoes this morning. I haven't made up my mind how to prepare them, but I want them clean when I return."

Brigitte, who disliked peeling the vegetables, was

happy with this assignment. Perhaps the potatoes would simply be baked in their jackets, requiring nothing more in preparation than a prick with a fork to let the steam escape. Her relief was short-lived. Dominique paused in the doorway. "I've decided. I'll mash them with a bit of butter and cream. So they must be peeled, too," she said. "Get Henri to help." Dominique suddenly stopped. "Where is Henri?"

"I haven't seen him, Aunt."

"Well, he is late." Dominique was frowning.

"Does he have far to come?" Brigitte suddenly realized how little she knew about Henri. He had never said where he lived. Of course, she had never asked.

"Well now, how should I know that?" Dominique answered. "As we told you on the day you arrived, I had hung out a notice that I was looking for help. He showed up on my door wanting a job. He said his father had been a cook, and it turned out the boy had some skill with food. That's all I cared—or care—about. But I must say, he is usually prompt. I wonder what's keeping him this morning?"

Just then Henri arrived at the café. "I'm sorry to be late, Madame. I had an errand to run this morning. As you know, we were here rather late last night."

"Close that door, boy—it's the end of November. You're letting all the warmth out." Dominique said.

Though the words were somewhat sharp, Brigitte noticed a smile creep around Dominique's mouth and she realized that her aunt was happy to see Henri. Nonetheless, Dominique was quick to add, "Your errands should be run on your own time, Henri," and when the young man opened his mouth, she held up a hand.

"Now, do not favor me with one of your pouts—or more of your famous excuses. There's no harm done. Just help Brigitte get these potatoes peeled before I return." And with that, Dominique, joined by Georges, who would be her basket-carrier, swept out of the café.

To Brigitte's surprise, the moody Henri seemed to take the reprimand rather easily. Eager to keep him happy, she said, "I'll wash, if you'll peel."

"That's best," Henri agreed. "You leave half the potato clinging to the jacket."

Brigitte sighed in frustration. "Let's not fuss this morning, Henri. I'm just too tired. I thought we would never close our doors last night. Is that why you were late? Did you sleep longer than usual?"

Henri looked at her with surprise. "Spoken like a spoiled child. Me? Sleep longer than usual? I have no time for that sort of bourgeois self-indulgence. I have work to do."

"Well, you weren't here on time to do it," Brigitte said, exasperated once again.

"Not this work. The work of my comrades."

"What comrades?" Brigitte asked. She hadn't seen a single friend of Henri's come into the café.

Henri looked at her and shook his head. "What comrades? Well, I am not going to divulge their names to the likes of you—that much is certain. But if you must know, I was with them this morning. They have important work for me; more important than anything at this café."

Brigitte stifled the impulse to dump the peelings bucket on top of his head. All she said was, "I think it would be wise to keep that opinion from Aunt Dominique, if I were you."

Henri settled himself on a stool and was testing the edge of the bone-handled knife against his thumb. Brigitte shuddered, remembering her own accident with it. "Be careful," she said.

"Well, how nice that you care."

Brigitte looked directly at Henri. "Don't be sarcastic. You might be surprised to know that I do care. You seem to think we're in . . . I don't know . . . some kind of contest. Who serves the tables best? Who peels potatoes properly? Well, who gives a fig? We're not competing for a prize."

"And what would any so-called prize be?" Henri said. "The café? As I've said, there's no contest there.

It's yours, no matter what I would do. And anyway, I don't want it."

"I wasn't even thinking about the café, but if it soothes you, you should know that I don't want it either. So that makes us even."

Henri did not respond. Brigitte scrubbed another potato in silence, then asked, "What *do* you want, Henri? You seem to have a talent for cooking. Dominique says your father was a chef. You said you rather liked Café Dominique. I thought that a café would appeal to you . . . that you might follow in your father's footsteps."

"My father with a café?" Henri laughed unpleasantly. "My father peeled potatoes and chopped carrots—for a circus. He was a cook, not a chef."

"A circus? How exciting! What circus?" Brigitte's thoughts immediately returned to the Medrano.

Henri looked at her as if she were dim-witted, and in a bitter voice said, "A small circus outside Moscow. He worked for a pittance, and when the circus moved on, he was left with nothing. No one cared that he had a wife and a small boy. No one cared that we were hungry. No one cared that we had no place to live. No one. Not the managers of the circus, not the people of the towns who paid good money to see the circus entertain them . . . no one. *No. One. Cared.*" Henri spat each word out as if his tongue had come upon a distasteful morsel of meat. "And you ask what I want? Nothing you or your aunt can give me, that much is certain. I want a change in society, and my comrades and I will bring it about."

Again, silence fell between them. Brigitte picked up the bucket of potato peelings that had accumulated and asked, rather timidly, "Who are your comrades and what changes are you talking about?"

Henri remained silent and brought his knife down to the cutting board with a savage blow. A piece of potato flew across the kitchen floor.

Brigitte hurried to pick it up and rinse it off. Then she tossed it into the pot with the others. "No harm done," she said, a false brightness in her tone. "Enough about comrades. What did you think of Apollinaire's opinion of *saltimbanques*? Last night, when he called them liars, I was shocked."

"Many of them are," Henri said dismissively. "Remember. I know circus people well."

"Do you think Paco is a liar?" Brigitte persisted.

"He could be." Henri answered. "But what of it? He is nothing, a *saltimbanque*. Yes, he's an outsider, just like Apollinaire said. A liar? Perhaps. But an artist? Hardly."

"Picasso seems to think *saltimbanques* are artists. He paints so many of them, and I know he and his friends love to go to the Medrano to watch them perform. I've heard them talk about lingering with the clowns after a performance, enjoying their company."

"Picasso. Now, there is someone of substance," said Henri, suddenly showing interest. "Picasso is bohemian. We share similar philosophies. We are beginning a new century. Everything is new. Art. Politics. Life. It's time for new friendships as well. Picasso and I will soon be friends."

"So that is why you rush to serve his table? You want to be his friend?" So that explained Henri's excessive attentiveness! A sudden sympathy rushed over Brigitte. Poor Henri. He was bound for disappointment. Picasso did not make friends easily—even she could tell that much.

"Henri, Picasso . . . well, Picasso is so . . . so changeable in his moods. You have seen how rude he can be—even to Fernande. You should be careful. I doubt he will become your friend. He seems content with his *bande* alone."

"Careful? Careful is for children." Henri shrugged. "I shall be bold, and I shall succeed. Picasso will become my friend—and thank me for it as well. You will see. As I said, everything is new. Everywhere."

Brigitte pondered Henri's statement. Parts of it were true. It was 1904, just weeks away from 1905. The century was new by anyone's standards. Her life—if not exactly new—was certainly not old, and it was definitely different from the life she had led in Poland. But Henri forging a new friendship with the curmudgeonly artist? She doubted that.

Nevertheless, her only comment to Henri was, "Well, try not to be disappointed if your efforts fail."

"They won't," the boy replied.

Chapter 10
THE DIPLOMAT

DOMINIQUE PUT THE FINISHING TOUCHES on the basket that Brigitte was to carry to Monsieur Pavlov's home. She inspected the napkin Brigitte handed her, and when she was satisfied that there was no evidence of a Picasso sketch, she spread it over the basket with a contented sigh.

"It's such a joy to me that a man of Pavlov's stature would come to my café. It's a pleasure to serve him— unlike some of my customers. He comes in, he reads his book or his newspaper, then he enjoys his meal, and afterward, his pipe. His table is quiet and refined. There are no arguments, no singing, and no giddiness. Just Monsieur Pavlov and his reading material."

"Well, he dines alone. It would be difficult for him to

sing and dance," said Brigitte, who was folding napkins.

Dominique peered at her closely. "Don't be a sassy girl," she said.

"I'm not being sassy, Aunt," Brigitte replied. "I just meant that if he talked, he would look silly since he is alone. Does he not have a family, or a companion?" It was time to change the subject.

Dominique paused. "I once heard him talk about a daughter back in Russia, but I seem to remember . . . I believe she may have died."

Brigitte felt a wave of sympathy for polite Monsieur Pavlov. "I have seen him linger after his meal, smoking his pipe, and I've wondered why he stays. Do you think he's lonely?"

"He could be," said Dominique. "He probably enjoys hearing some of the conversation that goes on at the other tables, though I am certain talk of art, circuses, and politics interests him only slightly. He is a man of real culture, and today's entertainments must bore him."

Monsieur Pavlov always looked very alert to Brigitte, not bored at all. Sometimes he jotted things down in a small notebook he kept in his vest pocket. Perhaps the conversations at the other tables interested him more than her aunt realized.

"How long has he been coming here?"

Dominique counted. "At least for the past six

months or so." She inspected the stack of napkins Brigitte had folded. Brigitte noticed that this time, she chose to refold only three of them. Dominique continued, "But we have only delivered Friday meals to him since late summer."

"Oh, he must have asked because he is so fond of your cooking, Aunt!"

Dominique allowed herself a small smile. "Well, of course. But to tell the truth, Monsieur Pavlov didn't ask for the deliveries. They were Henri's idea. Before you came, Henri always served Monsieur Pavlov, and he noticed that he never came to the café on Fridays. So the idea of taking a Friday meal to him came to Henri, out of the blue sky! Henri was so eager to make the deliveries. I'm afraid it was a serious disappointment to him that Monsieur Pavlov has now asked for you. I don't think he cares much for Henri, though I cannot for the life of me think why that should be."

I can, thought Brigitte.

The basket was ready. Dominique handed it over to Brigitte, saying, "Off you go. See that you don't linger too long outside the Medrano on your way back."

Brigitte's mouth flew open, and she started to protest.

"Never mind telling me you don't pass by there!" Dominique said. "I know you do. And I know you like to watch the monkey, the one that smiles—the one who leaped into our carriage the day you arrived."

"But how . . ."

"Dominique knows all. Dominique sees all!" said her aunt, waving her hands over an invisible crystal ball. Then she smiled. "I can see you do not believe me, so I shall reveal my secret. Fernande told me. She and Picasso have seen you there. Even though he paints seriously at night, apparently there are times he likes to sketch the rehearsals."

Brigitte was stunned. She had no idea that her little detours had been observed by anyone else, though when she considered it, why not? She had seen Picasso, more than once, sketching the Vela girls as they balanced on giant balls outside the tent, trying to lure paying customers inside. Picasso's eyes, so intense, did not miss a detail. And Fernande clearly loved to gossip. Of course she would have told Dominique.

"Ah, you wear a guilty look," Dominique said. "You needn't. But I don't want you lingering there too often. It . . . well, I don't like it, though Fernande has said you behaved with decorum. However, the crowd that gathers to watch the street show is a bit different from the one that pays to attend a performance. Those who pay are bourgeoisie—like we are."

Hope sprang up in Brigitte's heart. She hadn't dared broach the subject of actually attending the circus. She felt certain her aunt, in a fit of worry over her well-being, would forbid it. And now here she was, almost suggesting it! "Aunt, could I go to the circus someday? Someday soon? To see a real performance?" she begged.

"Well, we will see," said Dominique maddeningly. "Let me—" Brigitte leaned forward. Let her what? What?

"—get you a baguette to go with Monsieur Pavlov's lunch."

"Aunt Dominique!"

"Now hurry. Monsieur Pavlov is waiting. Watch the baguette as you walk, and be certain no crows attack it. Wave a napkin to keep them away—the pests!"

In an excess of good humor, Dominique suddenly exclaimed, "Montmartre is changing, my café is changing with the times, and more customers like Pavlov will soon crowd my tables, and I'll be rid of the ruffians. Please, Brigitte, be certain to give that good man my best regards."

As she headed for the diplomat's office, Brigitte thought about what Dominique had written to her mother: "*. . . if she works hard, the Café Dominique could one day belong to her.*"

But what if I don't want it, she thought, stepping carefully to avoid water running in the gutter of the street. Every day, Dominique was up at dawn and off to the markets to select the plumpest chickens, the leanest cuts of beef, as well as the day's supply of produce. Every day countless gallons of water were drawn from the well, and either Brigitte, Henri, Uncle Georges, or—at times—Dominique hauled the buckets into the kitchen. There were dishes to wash, fill with food, and then wash again. There were customers to please, and customers who, if wine had turned them from talkers into fighters, had to be asked to leave. Georges usually did that. Or Henri. Occasionally, there were customers who left before they paid their bill. When that happened, Dominique retired for the night with a cold cloth laid across her forehead—but not before she had thoroughly scolded Henri or Brigitte, whoever had served their table.

Monsieur Pavlov paid his bills without fail, so she couldn't blame Dominique for wanting to please him with the favor of these deliveries. Brigitte had to admit that the excuse to leave the café once a week and take a little time for herself was wonderful, but a few hours on a Friday afternoon did not amount to living the life she dreamed of. Where was the excitement and adventure? Brigitte's thoughts tumbled over each other in no particular order. *My mother wanted me to live—really live. She wanted me to do all the things she never got a chance to do. Is life at the café living?* The answer seemed obvious.

Chapter 11

THE PORTRAITS

AS BRIGITTE WALKED to the consulate, there was abundant evidence of the truth of her aunt's observation about Montmartre. The little village—along with Paris itself—was changing. New buildings were going up on each block, and stonemasons cut large blocks of stone for them, right on the spot. Glaziers walked down the street, each one carrying huge panes of glass on his back, calling out to see if anyone needed to repair a broken window or install a new one. The noise, the bustle, the sheer energy of building new things . . . Brigitte began to feel some of the excitement herself. Paris was growing and transforming itself, and she would grow and transform herself, too.

It wasn't too difficult to locate 97 Rue de Grenelle, but Brigitte was happy to see the small brass plaque out front that said "Russian Imperial Consulate." She felt a tingle of excitement as she lifted the heavy brass knocker and let it fall.

The housekeeper answered, but when Brigitte presented the basket, the older woman ignored it and instead led Brigitte into a large entryway. "Wait here," she said, and lumbered up a set of stairs that led to a landing and the second floor.

Brigitte stood, transfixed. She had never been inside a consulate before. The sheer size of the entrance hall made her feel small—and a bit uncomfortable. She stood, waiting for Monsieur Pavlov, shifting the heavy basket of food from one hand to the other, until she saw a long mahogany table lined up against a wall. She considered placing the basket on top of it, but then she thought better of the idea and put it on the floor, careful to avoid the Persian carpet in case something inside had leaked.

Monsieur Pavlov had still not come down, and Brigitte wondered what to do next. Should she leave? She'd been told to wait. But for how long? And who was a housekeeper to tell her to wait? She had delivered the man's lunch, and the Medrano and Toulouse were waiting for her. In a misery of indecision, Brigitte looked up at a series of large oil portraits that hung above the entrance hall table. Each painting depicted an elegant person in equally elegant clothes. Though she was not trained in art, Brigitte could tell that the paintings were very fine; every detail on the faces was carefully rendered. The skin tones glowed, each person's hair—smooth or curly—gleamed with painted highlights, every button on a uniform, every jewel around a neck, was painted with loving care. For a moment, Brigitte imagined herself in one of those lovely gowns, jewels around her neck, flowers tucked into her hair. *Soon*, she promised herself. *Soon I'll take care of myself, and who knows what my future will hold?*

"I see you are admiring our tsars, Brigitte. They are a fine-looking lot, are they not?" Monsieur Pavlov stood on the landing above, watching her.

Brigitte quickly picked up the basket. "They are, sir," she said. Then, not knowing what else to say, she added, "I've brought your lunch, Monsieur. Have a good afternoon." She dropped a small curtsy, and moved toward the door.

"Leave the basket there for a minute," Monsieur Pavlov said, coming down the steps to meet her. "I love to talk about these paintings, and I have so few visitors. Allow me to tell you about a few of them."

Brigitte's heart sank. The sidewalk show at the Medrano would be over before long. "The *coq au vin* is getting cold. It should be reheated." Brigitte said, hoping to distract the man and get on her way.

"Well, the housekeeper will do that if necessary,"

Monsieur Pavlov answered, taking Brigitte's elbow and steering her to the first portrait in the series—a handsome man in a military uniform.

"That, my dear, is Alexander II. He has been called 'the Tsar Liberator' because of the Emancipation Act of 1861. He gave the serfs their freedom."

Brigitte nodded, hoping she was looking interested. Another history lesson! She thought she had left those behind at Saint Stanislaus.

"And do you know how the people rewarded their great liberator?"

All Brigitte remembered or knew of Russian history was that its relations with its neighbor, Poland, had not been good. As a child, she had often fallen asleep in her mother's lap, listening to her father and grandfather discuss politics. Though she understood little of what was said, she understood enough to know that her father was not fond of Russia.

Monsieur Pavlov was looking directly at Brigitte, waiting for an answer to his question. She shook her head helplessly. "I'm sorry, Monsieur Pavlov. I don't know much history."

"Well, I shall tell you what the people did to their great liberator. They assassinated him," he said, his voice rising in emotion. "A student threw a bomb at him. Can you believe that, my dear? And women—girls, really—were involved in the plot."

Brigitte was shocked. She could imagine rough boys and men doing things like this, but girls? "Why would they kill someone who was trying to help them?" she blurted. It didn't make sense to her.

"People can be ignorant of what is best for them, my dear. Some of the serfs actually said they were worse off than they had been before they were freed. They remind me of the Israelites complaining in the wilderness after Moses convinced Pharaoh to set them free."

The only story about Moses that Brigitte could remember was the tale of him being found by Pharaoh's daughter, floating in a basket in the Nile.

"Why would anyone complain about being free?" Brigitte asked.

"The serfs simply could not cope with the responsibility of making their own decisions. They were like children—wanting freedom with no restraint. Others took advantage of that fact, and persuaded them the enemy was the tsar." Pavlov shook his head. "It is tragic. Alexander II felt he knew what was best, but now you know the results of too much freedom too soon." Monsieur Pavlov's tone had turned dark and bitter.

I'm something of a serf myself, Brigitte thought. *Everyone seems to know what's best for me. And if you have limits, you're not free—are you?* It was very confusing and Brigitte wanted to protest, but instead she murmured, eyes downcast, "I suppose so, Monsieur."

"Enough of this sad story. Come. There is more to tell."

Brigitte's heart sank in her chest. How much more to tell? Monsieur Pavlov had a grip on her elbow and was guiding her forward. Brigitte tried to pull her arm away discreetly, but the man's grip tightened as she moved. They stopped in front of another portrait, this one of an entire family.

"That's Nicholas II and his family. There is Tsar Nicholas, and the empress Alexandra, and their daughters, the grand duchesses Olga, Tatiana, Maria, and Anastasia. And there is Russia's future hope, their only son, the tsarevitch Alexei." Monsieur Pavlov's voice was warm with affection, as if he were pointing out members of his own family.

Brigitte thought of Monsieur Pavlov's dead daughter. He must have loved her like he seemed to love this family. She felt a wave of sympathy for him. Brigitte stared at the painting of the young royal family. They didn't look like the type of terrible people Henri had described. Not certain what was expected of her, she managed to say, "They look . . . nice."

Then she realized that Monsieur Pavlov, looking up at the painting and lost in thought, had finally loosened his grip on her arm. Quickly she picked up the basket of her aunt's food and asked, "This *coq au vin* will be ruined if you don't eat it quickly. Where will you be dining?"

Monsieur Pavlov shook his head as if to clear it. "Ah, these are working luncheons, my dear. Bring it in here." He led her into a room just off the entryway that clearly had been intended as the consulate's dining room, but appeared to have been converted into an office. The room was full of desks, tables, and cabinets. Brigitte unpacked the contents of the basket onto one of the desks as Monsieur Pavlov watched.

"How lovely of your aunt to provide this service when I cannot enjoy the camaraderie of the café. It is such a pleasure to be there," he said.

"Thank you, sir. My aunt appreciates your patronage and she looks forward to your visits," said Brigitte, carefully arranging the food.

"As do I," Pavlov said easily. "I particularly like to watch that young fellow sketch—what is his name again? The dark Spaniard, who wears the outlandish ties?"

"Oh, are you talking about Pablo Picasso?"

"Yes, that's the name. Mostly I hear him addressed as Picasso. I must say, he seems to sketch constantly, on anything that is available."

"He does," Brigitte agreed. "He even draws in the dirt, to amuse the neighborhood children. I saw him do that the day I arrived at the café. But I have to tell you—he also draws on my aunt's serviettes."

Monsieur Pavlov immediately picked up the white napkin that had covered the baguette.

"You won't find anything on it," said Brigitte, smiling. "It's my job to wash them. I use lye soap, and I get every trace of a drawing out. But if I don't watch, he'll draw on them again." Brigitte sighed.

"Well, I should say someone needs to teach that young bohemian some manners," Monsieur Pavlov said as he put the napkin back on the desk. "Tell me, does he—who does he talk to, at the café?"

Strange question, thought Brigitte. "His friends," she said cautiously.

"And who are his friends, my dear?"

Monsieur Pavlov had been at the café many, many times. He had seen Picasso there, and Picasso always came with the same companions, more or less. He knew Picasso's friends as well as she did . . . probably better.

"I'm not sure what you mean, sir . . ."

"What about that young waiter who works with you?"

"Henri?"

"Yes, so he calls himself. He seems to be friendly with the painter."

"I think Henri admires Picasso, sir. But friends? I doubt that very much. Picasso seems to care only for his *bande*, as he calls them."

"Well, I have seen him cast an admiring glance your way, my dear," Pavlov said.

True, Brigitte had squirmed uncomfortably a time or two when the artist had fixed her with his dark eyes and held her gaze as tightly as Monsieur Pavlov had gripped her elbow. Instinctively, however, Brigitte knew Dominique would not want her sharing any information about the café's customers with Monsieur Pavlov, so she said, "Oh, Monsieur, Picasso is quite the ladies' man. He is harmless, and it is best I say no more."

"Ah." Monsieur Pavlov's tone was different, more businesslike, less chatty and wheedling. "I see, my dear. I understand completely." Suddenly the iron grip was back on Brigitte's elbow, and he was steering her toward the door to the street. Once on the stoop, he pressed a few sous into her hand.

"This is more than enough to pay for the food, my dear. Be certain to tell your aunt I said you must have a generous tip. I've enjoyed our little visit. You are kind to indulge an old man and listen to his tales of the tsars." He turned and stepped into the consulate.

"Good-bye, Monsieur Pavlov!" she called, but the door had already closed.

Free! Brigitte skipped down the hill and over the few blocks to the Cirque Medrano. If she were lucky, the organ grinder would be outside, and Toulouse would be begging for coins. Brigitte had no extra coins to give, but she did have a few stale almonds that Dominique had tossed into the garbage. She reached in her pockets. Yes, they were still there. Brigitte smiled to herself. The organ grinder gets the coins from the crowd. It's time the little monkey gets a reward for his work, too.

Chapter 12

THE PAINTING

BY THE TIME BRIGITTE arrived at the Medrano, the free performance had come to an end. Her disappointment quickly turned to irritation—at Monsieur Pavlov. It was his silly history of the tsars that had made her late! She searched the thinning crowds, hoping Romero and Toulouse were still trying to wheedle a few last coins from a lingering bystander. Neither they, nor Paco, were anywhere to be seen.

Disappointed, Brigitte returned to the café, where she came upon her aunt and uncle arguing.

"Georges! Not another painting! How could you let him talk you into this? Or was it Fernande? The cheese seller tells me she can talk birds out of the trees, not to mention a wheel of Brie out of him. So, who made you take it? Fernande, or Picasso?"

Dominique did not wait for her husband to offer an answer before she went on. "Be reasonable, Georges. Are we to eat paper? Are we to use art to pay for eggs and onions? How can we run a profitable café if we are paid with paintings and not francs?"

Georges Boudoin stroked his chin, a certain sign he was uncomfortable. Brigitte felt a wave of affection for her kind uncle, always eager to please both his wife and his customers.

"Picasso pays when he can, dearest. But at the moment, he has no money and he asks that you accept this in payment for last week's meals. Please. He is our neighbor, as well as an artist. We should do this for him. He is hungry."

"And no wonder! Consider his art! Who would pay good francs for a portrait of a starving couple with hardly any food on their plate? So thin, so miserable!" Dominique was in a state. "You remember that painting. That was the one you took the last time he was in debt. Now I ask you—was that a picture for a café? I didn't know what to do with it. I certainly could not hang it out there." Dominique threw her arm toward the dining room.

"It was an interesting piece of art," said Georges, trying to defend the piece Dominique found so offensive. "It is an etching. Picasso told me he did it with a common household pin on a piece of zinc. And you are correct. There isn't much food on the couple's plate. Picasso called it *The Frugal Repast*—do you remember?"

"Well, no one has a frugal repast at the Café Dominique," Aunt Dominique said. "And his sad, pitiful couple certainly had money for wine—they look like alcoholics, if you ask me. I've stored it in the attic."

"You will grow to like it, Dominique," said Georges. "Everyone thinks he is a very inspired artist."

"Everyone, everyone!" said Dominique. "Who is everyone? His equally penniless friends? They think he is a great artist, because we take his paintings to pay their bills! What next? A poem from Apollinaire to pay for his *pot-au-feu*?"

Dominique picked up her favorite knife and began attacking a pile of potatoes. Georges and Brigitte looked at each other, relieved. The storm was ebbing— or so they thought.

"One more thing," Dominique said, waving the knife in the air like a weapon. "If we continue to extend credit to him, do you suppose he will be able to afford a color other than blue? Everything he paints is tinged with it. What kind of artist is that? And why does everyone he paints look so lonely? This is a new century. We should be happy—though I'm not too happy to be paid with paintings, I will tell you that. It's enough that I have to work so hard on all those napkins he destroys."

Brigitte tied on an apron. *I'm the one who cleans the napkins now,* she thought. Aloud, she said, "I hear them talk about art when I wait on their table, Aunt. They were talking about it just a few days ago. Picasso says that in his art, he does not seek. He finds."

"Finds! Finds a soft touch in your uncle Georges," scoffed Dominique.

"I think . . . well, I think what he finds is unhappiness. He is so poor! I hear all of them talking, complaining really. They say Picasso buys old paintings from junk dealers, just to paint over the canvas. And sometimes he cannot afford a single tube of white paint. How happy can he be?"

Brigitte paused for a moment, assessing whether to go on. When her aunt remained silent, she continued. "You know, Aunt Dominique, I know Picasso can be rude. But even though he seems surrounded with friends, I think he could be lonely, too. Perhaps he misses Spain. It's difficult to move from one place to another."

Dominique sighed with exasperation. "Well, you are in a new city, child, and you have adapted. So should he. And no one can be unhappy eating my cooking!"

"I am sure he is very happy here, Aunt, eating your good food," said Brigitte quickly, thinking how simple life was for her Aunt Dominique, who had never left the city in which she was born. Her aunt thought she had adapted. If she only knew how she longed for— for what? Something else, something exciting. Although the painter intimidated her, Brigitte also identified with Picasso, whose face lit with pleasure when Spanish friends joined him at the café and the conversation flowed easily in Catalan or Spanish.

Dominique interrupted her thoughts. "Ah, Brigitte," she sighed. "Let us hope you learn the restaurant business as easily as you seem to have learned what goes on in the mind of a painter."

Brigitte carried a pot of peeled and chopped rutabagas to the stove and poured a pitcher of water over them.

"Understand this," said Dominique, standing and stretching. "It doesn't matter a whit to me whether Picasso is happy, sad, or indifferent. Give me a rose that looks like a rose, or a mountain that looks like a mountain. For that matter, give me a person who looks like a person, not someone whose body has been stretched out like a piece of taffy, like those two miserable creatures who have little to eat. In art, as in life, things should be what they appear to be."

"Nothing is as it appears, my dear, in life or in art." Uncle Georges said with his usual good nature. "All this talk, and you still haven't seen the painting Picasso has given us. It's very special, and I think you will be happy. I dare say, you will hang this one where it can be noticed. It has very little blue in it."

"Hmmmf," Dominique said.

Georges hurried to fetch the painting, and Dominique shook her head, smiling slightly. "I see I have no choice in this, Brigitte. It seems another Picasso is going to clutter up my café."

Georges returned, and Brigitte saw a flash of blue as he pulled off the butcher paper it was wrapped in. *Oh dear*, she thought. Then Georges held the unwrapped picture in front of him, allowing both Dominique and Brigitte to see it together.

Brigitte was relieved to see that the blue she had seen was only the background. Against that background Picasso had painted a woman, her orange blouse—was it orange, or rose?—seemed to blend into the orange upholstery of the chair she sat upon. The face, which had been drawn in pencil, was clearly Dominique's. Brigitte peered more closely. Why, the skin was not painted at all! Picasso had allowed the white of the paper to provide the skin tone of the woman's face. Perhaps he had run out of white paint to make flesh tones.

Brigitte glanced from the woman in the painting to her aunt. The painting seemed to capture the essence of Dominique without trying to show a woman exactly like her. The painted woman had the same sandy-colored hair, the same angular face, and the same long slender fingers as Dominique—yet she was definitely different, a person in her own right.

As she took in the whole of the painting, Brigitte suppressed a smile. Picasso knew Dominique, and all her foibles. He was having fun with her. The woman in the painting was kissing a crow.

Dominique looked at the picture, then at her hands, as if to check the length of her own fingers. "I'll have to hang it somewhere, I suppose," she said with a sigh. "But the painting makes my point. Picasso does not paint what he sees. No one will ever, in this life or the next, catch me kissing a crow."

Chapter 13

THE HOLIDAYS

NOVEMBER SLID INTO DECEMBER, and Brigitte's life at the café fell into a rhythm. Mornings, she drew the first of several buckets of water from the well. Then she filled two large pots and set them on the stove to boil, ready for the day's cooking. It was Henri's job to gather logs from the pile of wood sitting outside and chop them into small pieces that would fit the stove's firebox, to be ready when the fire for the oven needed tending. After a few singed fingertips, and some holes in her apron, Brigitte had learned how to toss a piece of wood onto the fire with ease, avoiding the sparks that flew from the flames.

One evening in early December, when the last customer had left the café and Dominique had closed for the night, a weary Brigitte climbed up the stairs to her bed. No sooner had she put her head on the pillow and pulled the quilts up to her chin than there was a rap on the door, and it opened. Dominique stood there, a smile playing around her mouth.

"Brigitte! Where are your shoes? Have you forgotten what night this is? What would Père Noël say?"

In truth, Brigitte's new life was ordered by the days of the week, rather than the dates on the calendar. Mondays for washing; Tuesdays for folding and ironing; Fridays for deliveries to Monsieur Pavlov. She struggled to put a date to this Tuesday.

"Is it December sixth?"

"It is!" her aunt exclaimed. "Now you must get up and bring your shoes to the fire. It's the Feast of Père Noël."

"Is Père Noël the same as Saint Mikolaj?" she said sleepily, thinking about the saint whose holiday was celebrated in Poland on December sixth.

"One and the same," said Dominique, her eyes shining. "Now be a good girl. Get up and fetch your shoes."

Brigitte was tired, and her bed was warm. "I'm fourteen now, Aunt," she said. "I don't believe in Saint Mikolaj anymore."

"You don't believe? You don't believe?" said Dominique. "What would Père Noël say if he came to the Café Dominique tonight and did not find shoes by the kitchen fireplace? I won't stand for him thinking I have an unbelieving girl in my care. Now come, let us take your shoes downstairs."

Feeling foolish, and yet just a bit excited, Brigitte tossed off her quilt, picked up her brown leather ankle boots, and followed her aunt down the stairs. The bricks on the kitchen floor were icy on her bare feet, and Brigitte sped across the room to deposit her shoes on the fireplace hearth. Then she scurried back to the relative warmth of the wooden staircase, where she almost ran into her uncle Georges, who had come to watch.

"This will be the first time Père Noël has ever stopped at the Café Dominique," he said, putting an arm around his wife. "That is, *if* he stops. Have you been good, Brigitte?"

"What does it matter? There is no—" Brigitte started to answer. But then an image of her mother's delight in preparing for the arrival of Saint Mikolaj flooded her mind, and she stopped herself. When Brigitte was small, Sandrine had often started talking about the kindly saint's visit weeks before December sixth. She would tell and retell the story of the Polish bishop who visited good children on that day; if they put their shoes in front of the fire, he would fill them with fruit and nuts. Brigitte suddenly remembered that on one memorable December sixth, she had even found a special candy in her shoe—red and white, shaped into a shepherd's crook.

"It's the bishop's staff," her mother had explained. "Saint Mikolaj left it just for you. He wants you to remember that we give gifts, because the wise men gave gifts to the Christ Child."

Saint Mikolaj or Père Noël, it didn't matter. It had delighted her mother to give, and now it was Brigitte's turn to give back. She smiled at Uncle Georges and thought of her afternoon trips to see Romero and his monkey—and the few almonds she had "borrowed" from the nut bin. "I've only been rather good," she said. "Do you think that will be enough for Père Noël?"

Her aunt and uncle paused. Then her aunt, usually so sharp with her tongue, murmured, "Yes, I think that will be enough for Père Noël." Her voice caught, and she looked at her husband.

"I think it will be more than enough," said Uncle Georges.

Brigitte, on impulse, hugged first her aunt, then her uncle, and quickly ran up the stairs to bed.

The next morning, her boots were overflowing with fruit, nuts, and candy. And in the toe of one boot, there was a note in Dominique's careful script.

This is a promissory note for one ticket to the Cirque Medrano in the New Year 1905. Brigitte may choose the date.

Aunt Dominique and Uncle Georges

Brigitte could hardly contain her excitement. Her aunt had not forgotten her promise! At last! A chance to see a real performance at the Medrano! Brigitte tucked the precious note away and vowed to work cheerfully for the rest of December. 1905 was just around the corner.

On December twenty-fourth, the café closed early enough to allow Dominique, Georges, and Brigitte to attend midnight Mass at Sacré Coeur.

Brigitte and Henri were wiping the last few tables when Dominique came into the dining room, untying her apron. She surveyed the scene.

"Everything looks fine," she said. "I think we are finished for the evening. Brigitte, run up to smooth your braid, but don't undo it. We do not want to be late for Mass. We will have nowhere to sit."

Henri had begun to untie his apron. "You are most welcome to join us at Sacré Coeur, Henri. Would you come?" asked Dominique.

"I don't believe in anything like that," he said, hanging his apron near the door.

"What?" Dominique was shocked. It had never occurred to her that anyone would not believe in the catechism she had been taught since earliest childhood.

Henri smiled pityingly at Dominique. "Karl Marx says religion is the opiate of the masses."

"Well, I never heard of such a thing," said Dominique. "If I were you, I'd stop thinking about what this . . . this Marx person says. What does he know?" Dominique sniffed. "I shall have to pray for him. And for you."

"If it makes you feel better, please do so," said Henri. "As for me, I shall join some comrades tonight for an evening of cards and good talk. It is nice that the café is closed tomorrow."

Dominique fixed the boy with a steady look. "See that you are here bright and early on the twenty-sixth," she said. "We will have much work to do."

"Of course," Henri said as he stepped outside.

Dominique hurried to the door and called after him as he disappeared around the fountain in the square. "Henri!"

The boy turned.

"Merry Christmas!"

He bowed his head in a tiny salute and turned away into the cold.

<hr>

On January sixth, Dominique celebrated the last holiday of the Christmas season: Twelfth Night. Preparations had gone on for a week, as Dominique arranged circles of puff pastry and mixed and stirred rich almond filling to create her famous *galette des Rois*—the Kings' cake, named for the three wise men.

Picasso and his friends came into the café that evening, and Max Jacob insisted on ordering a *galette*. "Let us see who will have the luck in the New Year," he said as Brigitte brought the confection out from the kitchen. "Brigitte, put the plates in front of me. I shall do the honors."

"Brigitte, you are the youngest in the room," exclaimed Fernande. "You should choose who gets each piece!"

"I'm ready!" said Brigitte, laughing. As Jacob cut, she made a ceremony of walking around and around the table, starting to put a piece in front of Apollinaire, then snatching it away; giving it to Fernande, then reconsidering. . . .

At last everyone had a piece, and Brigitte waited to see which of them would find the charm— though "charm" was not the precise word for the tokens baked inside the café's cakes. To save money, Dominique—like many other thrifty cooks—had substituted a bean.

Picasso was happily devouring his piece, when suddenly his mouth twisted and his face pursed up as if he had eaten something sour. He spit a black bean into the palm of his hand, and when he saw it, the color drained from his face.

Before anything was said, Fernande clapped her hands. "Oh, Picasso is king—he got the charm!" She was beaming with excitement, and Brigitte, who had paper crowns in the pocket of her apron to crown the various "kings" among Dominique's customers that day, hurried to Picasso.

"I crown you king for the day, monsieur," she said as she laid a red paper crown over his thick black hair. "You will have good luck in 1905!"

Guillaume Apollinaire was watching closely. He elbowed Picasso jokingly and said, "Ah, you are such a superstitious Spaniard! What did you think? That the black bean meant death? Obviously you do not serve Kings' cake in Spain. The bean is good luck! What is it you are always saying? 'I am always doing that which I cannot do, in order that I may learn how to do it?' Well, my friend, you have despaired over your painting of the *saltimbanque* family, but trust my judgment: you have learned how to capture the loneliness of the circus. *Family of Saltimbanques* will be your masterpiece of 1905, and the black bean merely confirms it. May you have many sales in this new year!"

"Hear, hear!" Everyone at the table lifted a glass in solidarity with Apollinaire's prediction. Picasso reached up, adjusting the crown on his head so that it tilted at a rakish angle, falling down over one eye, just as his lock of hair always did. And then he smiled. He lifted his glass with the others.

"*Salud!*" everyone exclaimed together.

Chapter 14

THE PERFORMANCE

"MIND YOUR POCKETBOOK, and watch where you sit. Montmartre is not the nice little village it used to be. There are pickpockets and thieves everywhere, so keep your wits about you," Dominique said as she handed Brigitte a small purse. "There should be enough money here to buy a sweet, as well as your ticket. Don't try to walk back up the hill at night. Take the funicular." The older woman hesitated, worry etched on her face. "Oh, dear. I do hope I haven't made a mistake. Would your mother have allowed you to attend a circus?"

"I will, I will! She would! She would!" cried Brigitte, leaving it to her aunt to decipher what she was responding to. "And . . . thank you, Aunt."

"Have a good time," said Dominique, reaching under Brigitte's scarf to smooth her hair. "You have been working very hard and have shown yourself to be quite responsible. It is good to enjoy yourself a bit. Live your life, my dear!"

Startled, Brigitte stared at her aunt. It could have been her mother talking. "I will," Brigitte said fervently, then added a last "thank you" as she clutched her wool cloak around her and stepped into the cold winter night. She could hardly believe it was finally happening: she was going to the circus to see a real performance—not just the free ones performed on the street.

When Brigitte reached the Medrano, she moved through the crowds, heading for the ticket kiosk. She concentrated on keeping her purse close to her side, ever on the watch for the dreaded pickpockets that so worried her aunt. Intent on her task, Brigitte almost missed seeing Paco, who was doing his tricks, encouraging laggards to buy their tickets and come inside. When he saw Brigitte, the *saltimbanque* did a final somersault, then walked over to her.

"So, you came to the Medrano at last. I was certain you would never be allowed."

"Of course I'm allowed," Brigitte answered, eager to appear as someone who made her own decisions. "My ticket is a gift—from Père Noël." She tried on the kind of smile she had seen Fernande use on Picasso— one that said, "See what a coquette I can be?"

"Père Noël? Père Noël is for children."

Brigitte's cheeks turned crimson. "Well, I don't *believe* in Père Noël," she said quickly. "But Aunt Dominique insisted that I put my shoes in front of the fire. I did it to please her." The words came out in a rush.

"Of course," Paco answered, smiling slightly. The look he gave Brigitte told her he was not at all certain she had left that childhood fantasy behind.

Brigitte craned her head to see behind Paco. "Have you seen Romero and Toulouse? I saved some nuts from my shoe for him."

"Romero, or Toulouse?" Paco was smiling more broadly now.

"Paco, don't be such a tease," Brigitte said, fervently wishing the teasing would never stop. "I'm bringing the nuts to Toulouse, of course. Now where are they? They weren't here the last time I came by, either."

Paco's face turned serious, and he let out a small sigh. "I don't know what is happening . . . something is odd. Toulouse is around somewhere, moping. Romero seems to have gone away, for the first time ever, and the monkey doesn't like it at all. A lot of strange things are going on. Why, Picasso was here this morning, sketching some of the performers. He has done so before, of course. But he usually works at night."

Brigitte, eager to keep the conversation going, feigned interest in Picasso. "Really? Well, I only see him at the café. Fernande told Dominique . . ." Before she finished the sentence, Brigitte realized she didn't want to discuss her own furtive visits to the afternoon performances. It embarrassed her to think that Paco had seen her there, as well as Fernande. Instead, she said, "I thought Picasso was working hard, every minute."

Paco nodded. "I was surprised to see him here. He was up all last night, putting final touches on the painting that I pose for—the *saltimbanques*. But enough of the painter," Paco said, abruptly changing the subject. "Come. Buy your ticket. Then look for me in the performance. If you'll wait after the show, I'll meet you by the center ring. We can talk more then."

"I have to get home—" Brigitte started to say, then hastily added, "—before it gets very late."

"Until later, then," Paco said. "You must excuse me now." As if by magic, he disappeared into the tangled crowd.

The tent was filling rapidly now, and the atmosphere inside was charged with excitement. Brigitte's skin tingled, and she took deep breaths to still her pounding heart. She had a very good seat, right in front of the center ring. She closed her eyes, letting her emotions wash over her. *I'm here—I'm really here.* For a moment, she felt her mother's presence so intensely that she half-expected to see Sandrine sitting next to her when she opened her eyes again. Instead, the seat was occupied by a small French woman, accompanied by a very large man. Brigitte, centered again in reality, managed a small smile.

The circus band struck up a lively march, and the center ring rapidly filled with a line of brightly costumed performers, walking, riding, and tumbling in a glorious parade. The clowns led their dogs, making them jump through hoops and dance on two legs. Men and women stood on the bare backs of galloping horses, holding the reins lightly, as they balanced first on one leg, then the other. The *saltimbanques* tumbled and flipped their way around, occasionally standing on one another's shoulders, as the parade passed by in a whirl of color and noise.

Brigitte strained to catch a glimpse of Paco. There were so many *saltimbanques*, she wondered if she would recognize him. Yes! There he was! He was walking on his hands once again. Then he turned himself upright and began to move around the ring in a series of cartwheels that appeared so easy and graceful Brigitte longed to try them herself.

Through it all, a tall man with a mustache, dressed in a red coat and a black silk top hat, stood in the center of the ring, brandishing a whip and announcing the acts as they paraded by.

It only seemed like minutes to Brigitte before the parade was over. The last horses pranced out of the ring. Paco and the other *saltimbanques* gave their final flips and cartwheels, waved to the audience, and disappeared backstage. The ringmaster blew a whistle and cracked his whip. The show was ready to begin!

"La-a-a-dies and gentlemen, boys and girls, welcome to the Cirque Medrano! So many exciting acts tonight, unequalled under any big top! First I draw your attention to the center ring, where you will watch our lovely Miss La La risk her life and her limbs to entertain you, as she performs Mazeppa's Ride, made famous in the poem by Lord Byron. To remain true to the situation of the unfortunate gentleman who inspired the poem—and henceforth, the trick—Miss La La will be strapped atop this wild beast completely unclothed!"

The ringmaster paused for the collective intake of breath that went through the tent, then continued to build the anticipation. "Ladies and gentlemen, this trick is extremely dangerous. For the safety of Miss La La and the entire audience, I must ask that you remain silent."

Brigitte gulped. She could tell her cheeks had turned scarlet. Her aunt had often talked about the bohemians of Montmartre, but she had not thought Mazeppa's Ride would be this risqué. Briefly, she thought about leaving. But only briefly.

"Will the straps break? Will the beautiful Miss La

La be thrown to the sawdust? Will she be trampled underfoot? Who knows?"

Brigitte remembered what her Uncle Georges had said when they discussed the circus on her first day in Paris. "People get hurt . . ."

With a crack of the ringmaster's whip, the band started playing again. The lights in the tent dimmed, and the music faded into the lone sound of a drum roll. Two trainers struggled to hold a huge white horse that threatened to break their grasp. The girl strapped to its back looked pitifully small.

Suddenly, as the drum roll built to a climax, the horse began to gallop and rear around the center ring, spurred on by the crack of the ringmaster's whip. Had the trainers released it on purpose? Had it simply broken away from them? Brigitte was on the edge of her seat, afraid to look, afraid to look away.

The crowd clapped as Miss La La rode around the ring, her body whipped about by the horse's fury, as if she were some kind of rag doll.

Brigitte had told herself not to look when Miss La La rode by—but in the end, she couldn't resist a peek. She was relieved to see that the straps securing Miss La La to her horse looked extremely strong. And something was flapping around on her body, giving away the fact that Miss La La was not "completely unclothed" but wearing a flesh-colored body suit.

Miss La La completed her ride without catastrophe. The trainers "caught" her horse, released the straps that bound her, and Miss La La, none the worse for wear, took her bow. Brigitte noticed that the horse seemed amazingly docile as Miss La La led it out of the tent. So, everything in the circus was not what it was advertised to be. Despite herself, Brigitte felt a twinge of disappointment.

There was a pause in the performance as circus hands scurried about, stretching a heavy net across the center ring. The crowd buzzed in anticipation. The man on her left whispered to his wife, "Hmmmf . . . they're using a safety net! I should get our money back."

Brigitte looked at him with what she hoped was a disapproving glare.

"Ladies and gentlemen, direct your attention overhead for our next act," called the ringmaster. Brigitte looked up obediently and felt a bit dizzy gazing into the bright lights and web of ropes attached to the top of the tent.

"Prepare to witness the death-defying trapeze artistry of Anna Maria de Suarez!" Brigitte sat forward in her seat. She had not thought of Paco's younger sister since her first day in Paris, when Henri pointed her out in the crowd. Paco had mentioned his little sister from time to time, so Brigitte knew she posed for Picasso's "masterpiece," too. Nevertheless, the child had never come to the café—at least, not when Brigitte was there, which was practically all the time. Now Anna Maria was going to perform!

The spotlight picked out a young girl standing in the sawdust of the center ring. She was dressed in a lacy black top and flowing pink skirt. Brigitte remembered it from her first day in Paris, when the carriage stopped for a while and Henri pointed her out. Anna Maria's hair was piled on top of her head, pinned there with a red rose. She stood perfectly still, as an iron ring attached to a long velvet-covered rope was lowered from the top of the tent. The ring stopped right in front of her face.

After several salutes to the crowd, the girl opened her mouth and clamped her teeth down on the ring. Brigitte watched, absentmindedly rubbing her lower jaw, which—along with her teeth—had begun to ache. Slowly, slowly, tiny Anna Maria was hoisted to the top of the tent, the muscles in her cheeks bulging with the effort to hang onto the ring. The audience gaped in silence. At the top of the tent, she maneuvered herself onto a tiny platform and finally dropped the ring from her mouth, bringing forth thunderous applause from the audience, which she acknowledged with a graceful wave.

Brigitte imagined herself standing there, waving to an audience. Inconspicuously, she practiced an open-handed wave, keeping her hand close to her lap.

Excitement washed through her, and she looked back at Anna Maria.

The spotlight had moved from Anna Maria to another performer, waiting on an opposite platform. Brigitte drew in her breath. It was Paco! She had no idea he also did trapeze work. Paco saluted the crowd, then sent the slender bar of the trapeze sailing across the tent to his sister. Anna Maria caught it with both hands and jumped from her tiny platform in one fluid movement. Brigitte gasped.

Anna Maria began to swing, pumping her legs to make the trapeze arc higher and higher. The circle of light grew wider and wider, then moved and narrowed to focus on Paco.

Paco, sitting on his own trapeze, saluted the crowd with one hand, and swung out over them. Brigitte sat in rapt attention. In one deft movement, Paco dropped from his sitting position to one in which he hung by his knees. Brigitte felt her stomach leap. The audience whooped. Paco and Anna Maria swung past each other, each one taking riskier and riskier holds on the slender bars that were all that kept them from falling. Brigitte felt faint and yet excited. This was Paco—the boy who was meeting her after the show—flying across the top of the tent! She tried to swallow and noticed that her mouth was as dry as the sawdust on the floor.

The music began to fade, and once more there was

the ominous sound of a drum roll. Once more the ringmaster asked the audience for silence. Brigitte felt as if the crows that so loved her aunt Dominique's baguettes were beating their wings inside her chest.

Anna Maria gave her trapeze a few more vigorous pumps and then flew off it, contorting herself into a series of somersaults as she tumbled through the air, arms extended, reaching for Paco, who hung by his knees, swinging toward his sister, waiting for the catch.

The next seconds were a blur.

Anna Maria's body twisted, and instead of grabbing both her wrists, Paco only managed to get hold of one. There was a shriek of pain, a collective gasp from the audience, and Anna Maria plummeted into the net below.

For a moment, the entire tent was silent as Anna Maria lay there, stifling sobs. There was a hesitation in the audience, as if they didn't know quite what was expected of them. A few booed as Anna Maria was helped out of the net and onto the floor. Gamely, she raised her uninjured arm. Brigitte stood and began clapping, and soon the entire audience joined in.

Brigitte's palms were still tingling from the effort when the spotlight drew the audience's attention back to Paco, who had returned to his platform when Anna Maria fell. Another drum roll, and Paco swung onto his trapeze once again. Then, in a quick series of spectacular midair somersaults, he landed first in the safety net, flipped off it, and landed on the floor of the center ring, throwing up both hands in a gesture of victory, before he hurried off in search of his sister. The crowd went wild, applauding and cheering.

For Brigitte, the acts that followed went by in a blur. She could not take her mind off of what had just happened. As Anna Maria left the ring, Brigitte saw that the child's face had turned the color of one of Dominique's napkins after a good wash. Paco had looked—what? Worried? Even angry?

When the last act had ended, Brigitte quickly made her way toward the center ring, pushing through the laughing, talking throng moving in the opposite direction toward the exit. Fifteen minutes later, Brigitte's hand was still firmly planted on her purse as she stood, waiting for Paco. It was getting late, and most of the crowd had left. She knew she should be going home. Dominique would be expecting her. *Oh well,* she thought, *I can explain. And even if I can't, I'm old enough to take care of myself.*

The back flap of the huge pink tent was open now, and through it, Brigitte could see clusters of clowns talking together. She squinted to see more clearly. Was that Picasso among them? It was! He, Fernande, and the rest of his friends from the café must have watched the show, and now they were sharing jokes with the performers. Fernande saw Brigitte and raised her hand in greeting. Brigitte waved back, silently praying that Fernande would keep this chance sighting to herself and resist the temptation to share this piece of information with Dominique, who would not approve of lingering.

The Bearded Lady walked by outside and, to Brigitte's amazement, reached up and gently worked the hair right off her chin as she headed toward her tent. Brigitte had to smile. Things at the circus weren't always what they seemed. The Bearded Lady saw Brigitte's look of good-natured surprise and let out a laugh, and waved. Brigitte, happy to be included in this small gesture, called out. It was a giddy feeling, being out in the evening by oneself. The Bearded Lady had waved to her, Paco was coming to meet her—why, she was almost a part of the circus! Brigitte's imagination took flight. She was part of the circus, a star. People stared up at her as she swooped across the tent in a series of graceful arcs on her trapeze. Paco was swinging toward her, and she didn't miss his grasp. They smiled at each other. Now that was truly living! She glanced around the tent to be certain she was alone, then raised her hand and practiced a wave.

As she did so, Brigitte realized that the tent was empty and the audience was gone. Through the open flaps she could see small campfires dotting the fairgrounds. The scent of burning charcoal filled the night air. Various circus performers drifted toward their families, and unwelcome thoughts of Dominique waiting for her at the café came flooding back, destroying the happy thoughts of a moment earlier.

Uncertainty washed over Brigitte, and she considered running back to the security of the known world of the Café Dominique. But it was as if her feet had grown roots, and she was planted in the sawdust, unable to move. She stood still, waiting for Paco. *I can do this*, she told herself. *I can wait for Paco and explain myself to Aunt Dominique later. And anyway, this is where I belong.*

She put her hands in her pockets to warm them, and felt the nuts that she had saved for Toulouse. Idly, she wondered if Romero had returned. There was no sign of either the organ grinder or his monkey, and Brigitte cracked a chestnut under her heel and ate the meat herself. Then she yawned and sighed, wondering how much longer she dared wait.

At last he appeared.

"I am sorry I kept you waiting. I hope you understand. I had to see about Anna Maria. There's been some trouble. Her arm—it is broken. She will not be able to perform for many weeks."

"How terrible! Is she in much pain?" Brigitte hoped the weariness was not showing in her face.

"A bit, but she is resting now," Paco said. "Brigitte, I had planned to walk you back to your aunt's café, but now I must go straight to Picasso's studio. I pose tonight."

"Do not give it a thought," Brigitte said, hoping she sounded like someone who did not need to be escorted home. "I will take the funicular. I can take care of myself."

Chapter 15

THE APPLES

THE FOLLOWING MORNING, Brigitte sat in the empty dining room, folding a stack of napkins. Unlike chopping vegetables, this task had no inherent danger, and Brigitte was free to dwell on the events of the evening before. The performance had been so enthralling! She relived the acts, the sights, the sounds—even the smell of peanuts combined with manure seemed like exotic perfume. Afterward, Paco had been so sweet, so kind and concerned that she get home safely. The *saltimbanque's* face swam up in her imagination—his short, close-cropped hair, his bright blue eyes. She allowed herself a happy sigh as she carried the neat stack of napkins to the buffet for storage.

A noise from the kitchen made her look up in time to see Henri hanging his coat on a peg, and her

lighthearted mood changed quickly. Henri was so . . .
"difficult" was the word that came to mind

Brigitte's thoughts were interrupted by Monsieur
Dubroq, the greengrocer whose shop was next to
the café.

"Stop, thief! I saw you take that apple!" he was
yelling. "I saw you with my own eyes! Now give it back."

Eager to see the commotion, Brigitte wiped her
hands on her apron and hurried through the door of
the café in time to see Anna Maria standing in front of
the grocer, frozen in her tracks by his ranting. An apple
was just visible inside the dirty canvas sling that sup-
ported her injured right arm. The girl reached inside,
fished the apple out, and took a large bite before offering it back to the indignant grocer.

Despite herself, Brigitte laughed out loud. Anna
Maria's nerve impressed her—but it did not impress
the grocer, whose ears grew dangerously red.

"You dirty little circus brat! You're all a pack of
thieves!" he said.

"I'll replace your apple with one from my aunt's
kitchen, if you like, Monsieur Dubroq," said Brigitte.

"Oh, so you'll steal, too, is that it?" said the man,
quivering in his indignation.

"I don't think my aunt would mind," said Brigitte,
not entirely certain that statement was true, and
thereby adding to her list for confession on Friday.

Dubroq, who had sold many a bushel of produce to Dominique Boudoin, had no interest in involving the café in this incident. Shaking his head, he marched into his store and returned with a small three-legged stool, which he placed directly in front of his outdoor display of fruits and vegetables. He glared at Anna Maria and sat down, crossing his arms over his chest. Brigitte watched with some amusement. *Dubroq defends his produce as some defend their children*, she thought.

Anna Maria walked away, still eating the apple, and Brigitte called out, "Wait! Anna Maria, wait!" She hurried toward the girl, and when they were side by side, Brigitte paused, expecting Anna Maria to say something. When the girl continued to eat her apple and eye Brigitte sullenly, Brigitte asked, "What? No thanks for defending you?"

"I don't need anyone to defend me," said Anna Maria, tossing her head. "I was hungry. And how do you know my name?"

"I know your brother, Paco. My name is Brigitte. I work at the café."

Brigitte studied Anna Maria, who had now chewed the apple down to its core and was sucking out the remaining juice and spitting the seeds deftly onto the dirt. Clearly the girl thought her hunger rationalized everything.

"Don't spit those seeds there," Brigitte said. "My aunt works hard to keep the café respectable."

Anna Maria shrugged, but she stopped spitting the seeds.

"You should have paid for that apple," Brigitte said. "Dubroq could have called the gendarmes, you would have been taken to jail, and then what would you have done?"

"My brother would have come for me," the girl said defiantly. "He would have found me." Despite Anna Maria's bravado, tears escaped and rolled down her dirty cheeks, leaving clean tracks behind.

"Come, sit with me," Brigitte said, taking Anna Maria's good arm and steering the girl to one of the café's empty outdoor tables—the one farthest away from Dubroq and the temptations of his fruits and vegetables. "If I go inside and get you a piece of bread and some cheese, will you be here when I return?"

Anna Maria nodded wordlessly.

As Brigitte walked into the café's kitchen, she saw Henri was in the backyard, by the wood stack. He was talking animatedly to a man, and Brigitte peered through the window to get a better look. Who was he? The figure was familiar, and when he turned to leave, she saw him. It was Romero, minus his barrel organ and Toulouse. She was certain of it. She ran toward the backyard, but Henri was already at the door, coming inside, and they almost collided.

"Oh. Sorry," Brigitte said. "I was hurrying to ask you. Was that Romero you were talking to?"

"And if it was?"

"Nothing. I just know some people at the circus have been worried about him. Toulouse misses him."

"Did you hear that?" Henri asked, addressing the empty space in the kitchen, his hands uplifted in mock wonder. "The child worries about a monkey!" He looked at Brigitte directly and said, "I have to go to the root cellar to fetch turnips."

"Was that Romero?" Brigitte insisted, but Henri had already disappeared down the steps.

Suddenly, Brigitte remembered Anna Maria. Was she still waiting for her bread and cheese? Brigitte put a round of goat cheese and half a baguette on a plate and hurried outside, where Anna Maria—true to her word and to Brigitte's surprise—had waited. Brigitte put the plate in front of the girl and took a seat, eager to watch the child enjoy her meal. But Anna Maria didn't touch her food, though it was obvious she was hungry.

Brigitte continued to watch in silence, until a thought occurred to her. "Are you right-handed?" she asked.

Anna Maria nodded.

116

"I see. Well, with that sling, I suppose it's difficult to spread the cheese. I can do it for you. Or you can take it home with you, if you'd like."

"I'll take it home," Anna Maria immediately replied. "I can give some to Mother and Manuel."

"I didn't realize you had . . ." Brigitte was going to say "a mother" and caught herself in time. "A little brother. Paco didn't mention him."

"His name is Manuel. He's six. I'm ten."

Brigitte watched Anna Maria devour a small piece of the bread and cheese, and nodded.

"You're small for your age."

Anna Maria's scowl told Brigitte the comment had been a mistake, and she hurried to make amends. "Oh, but now that I look more closely, I can see you are ten. Does Manuel perform with the circus, too?" It was best to change the subject.

"He tries," Anna Maria said. "But he's sick, so he can't work very much. I don't want to talk about him anymore."

"Very well. Let's talk about something else. I loved watching you last night, though I hated to see you fall. How does your arm feel?"

Anna Maria shrugged. "It feels better in the sling, but I can't fly anymore. Not until it gets better. Now they want me to try the Spanish web. Paco says I should be ready for that in a few more days."

At the sound of Paco's name, Brigitte felt a danger-ous thump in her chest. "What's the Spanish web?" she asked, hoping her face had not turned red.

"You wrap yourself in a soft rope that hangs from the top of the tent, then you do poses in the air, but you never let go completely. The rope is always wrapped around you, and it has loops for your hands, so unless you miss your grip, or it comes unwound, you won't fall. It's not as dangerous as trapeze work."

"That sounds very nice," said Brigitte. "But not as nice as flying through the air!"

Anna Maria looked at Brigitte. "What do you know about flying through the air?" she said, rather rudely.

"Not much," Brigitte admitted. "But I was inspired by your bravery last night. And I think it looks like . . . well, like fun. If you don't fall, of course," Brigitte added quickly. "It's probably best that you do this . . . this Spanish web for now. It must be safer for you."

Anna Maria studied her solemnly. "Are you com-ing to the circus again?" the girl asked. "If you do, you can see me do it. After I've practiced."

Silence fell for a moment as Anna Maria gnawed on the round end of the baguette. "Paco is mad at me now," she said quietly, changing the subject.

"Mad at you? Why?" Brigitte was astonished. Paco had seemed so concerned about his sister.

"The director of the circus called him in, right after the show."

Brigitte remembered how long she had waited for Paco and how worn out he had seemed.

"Lars told Paco he was thinking of getting rid of our act," said Anna Maria.

"Oh, no!" cried Brigitte. "You were wonderful! The best part of the show! He should allow you to do the Spanish web, and wait for your arm to heal."

"That is not Lars's way," said Anna Maria simply. "If you perform and the crowds like you, you stay. If you are hurt, or tired, or too young, or too old to go on, out you go. If he fires us, we'll be travelers again."

"What are travelers?" Brigitte asked.

"It's the name for circus people who keep moving—doing our tricks by the side of the road for anyone who will give us coins. That's how we worked our way from Spain up to France—Manuel and me, my mother and Paco. We were happy to be able to stay here, at Cirque Medrano. At least we pitch our tent and leave it pitched. It's much easier to live in one place than to move around all the time."

Anna Maria gave Brigitte a surprisingly sweet smile. "Why are you talking to me, anyway? Most townies don't talk to circus people. Most are like the grocer over there." Anna Maria tossed her head in the direction of the shopkeeper, who was busily extolling the virtues of his beets to a potential customer. "They think we're all pickpockets and thieves."

"Well . . . you did take his apple," said Brigitte.

Anna Maria started to gather up the bread and cheese with her left hand.

"Wait, wait. Listen to me. I will say nothing more about the apple. Tell me . . . you speak a different language than I am used to. Travelers. Townies. Let me guess. A townie is someone who lives in town—yes?"

Anna Maria nodded. She settled down again and managed to tear off more of the bread, eating it despite her intention of taking it home.

"Well, I'm a townie, and I talk to circus people," said Brigitte.

Just then Paco came into the square. "There you are!" he said as he approached his little sister. "I've been looking for you. You need to return to the circus for practice."

"I'm coming, I'm coming!" said Anna Maria. She jumped up, but she seized on this opportunity to ask her brother a favor. "Can Brigitte come to watch me on the Spanish web? Tonight? After the performance?"

Paco looked at his sister, and his face grew stern. "She can, if we're still there after tonight's performance. You know how angry Lars is, Anna Maria. Now you'd best get back and get to work."

Anna Maria rose from the chair, and something rolled out of the sling on her arm. With a quick movement, Paco caught it before it hit the ground. Another apple.

"What's this?" Paco said. He polished the apple on his shirt before starting to take a bite.

"Don't eat that," Anna Maria cried. "I was getting it for Manuel."

"She was *taking* it for Manuel," Brigitte corrected, putting her hand on Anna Maria's shoulder to soften her words. She spoke softly, so Dubroq and the passersby would not hear. "The grocer almost called the gendarmes."

Paco shook his head. "You got caught, Anna Maria? How many times do I have to tell you? If you're going to steal, don't get caught."

Brigitte could hardly believe her ears. How could Paco talk this way? "She shouldn't steal at all," she protested.

"She's hungry." It was a simple statement, uttered as if it explained everything. The winter sun disappeared behind a cloud, and Paco's mood darkened with the sky.

"Do you think we have a kitchen like the one in this café? Do you think there are pots of soup, and plates of chicken, and cheese, and bread, waiting for us after every performance? No. We have little to eat. The grocer will not miss one or two apples."

"Well, obviously, he did," said Brigitte. Paco's words stung, and she was angry. It was not her fault that she had plenty to eat, and it still wasn't right for Anna Maria to steal.

Suddenly Henri stepped outside. "Spoken like a true member of the bourgeoisie," he said with a hint of sarcasm. Brigitte wanted to scream—he must have been right inside the window, listening to everything.

"I am not bourgeoisie!" Brigitte protested. The conversation in the café—especially among the members of Picasso's *bande*—seemed to indicate that being bourgeoisie was a fate worse than death. If Picasso, Apollinaire, and even the glamorous Fernande, disdained the middle class, then there must be something wrong with it.

Henri looked at the apple that Paco was holding, and he smirked. "The apple does not fall far from the tree, Brigitte. Your aunt and uncle are members of the bourgeoisie, and you are, too. You say please and thank you, and you obey all the rules. You don't think of the poor and the powerless. You probably are looking forward to running this café some day, where you will continue to cook, clean, and amass money, and that makes you a member of the bourgeoisie."

Anna Maria spoke up timidly. "I think that sounds nice. What's wrong with it?"

"We are artists, Anna Maria," Paco said. "We are

part of *la bohème*—just like Picasso. But even bohemi-ans must practice their art—and that means you, little sister. Now get back to the Medrano and let Lars see you hard at work. I have some business to tend to." He pushed open the door of the café and went inside.

Henri gave Brigitte a last look before he followed. "We are not shopkeepers or merchants, like Dubroq over there, constantly worrying if someone will steal his apples," said Henri.

"Oh, no?" said Brigitte. "Before I came, you were happy to be here, working at the café. You were a shopkeeper then. What are you now?"

"I was never a shopkeeper. I don't own this café—your aunt owns it," said Henri. "For now."

"What are you talking about—for now? Aunt Dominique will own this café forever."

"There will come a time when things change for your kind. Just wait. You will see," Henri said ominous-ly. "You should listen to the bohemians . . . they know." Bewildered, Brigitte stepped back, and Henri turned and stalked into the café behind Paco.

Brigitte suddenly realized she had backed into Anna Maria. The younger girl was clutching her shoulder with her good hand.

"Owww!" Anna Maria yelped.

Brigitte was horrified. "Oh! I'm so sorry. Are you all right?"

"I'm fine," Anna Maria replied. "But I think I should go now. Paco told me to go home and practice. My mother must be waiting for me—I will go," Anna Maria stammered. As she walked away, Anna Maria looked back over her shoulder at Brigitte. "The next time you come to the circus, I'll show you the Spanish web."

Brigitte felt a rush of excitement. Never mind Henri and his crazy ideas! She was going to go behind the scenes at the circus! "You will? Do you promise? Thank you!" she called as Anna Maria left the square, tossing her thoroughly chewed apple core onto the ground. The crows that so plagued Dominique as they scrounged from patrons would soon be upon that choice morsel.

Brigitte walked over and picked it up.

Chapter 16

THE PHILOSOPHIES

WHEN BRIGITTE RETURNED to the dining room to clear tables, she saw Henri hovering around the table where Picasso was dining. Paco stood nearby, waiting for the painter to finish his meal. Henri was fawning over Picasso, who ignored his attentions for a while; then when it seemed to be just too much, the artist waved his hand at the boy, as if he were shooing away a fly.

Observing the exchange, Brigitte saw the expression on Henri's face darken. Abruptly, he brushed past Brigitte and headed toward another table. *He knows I saw Picasso dismiss him,* Brigitte thought. *Poor Henri. Despite his flatteries, Picasso doesn't seem to like him at all.*

Picasso pushed back from the table and rose to leave, but not before saying something to Fernande, who in turn spoke in a quiet voice to Paco, who nodded agreement.

As the party left the café, Paco lingered. He called to Picasso, "So I will see you in the studio in a half hour."

Picasso lifted his hand in acknowledgment as he left the café, and Brigitte approached the now-empty table with her clearing tray.

"If you're looking for a tip from Picasso, there isn't one," Henri said. "He's exploited, like me."

Brigitte felt her anger well up. "Does my aunt exploit you, Henri? Is that what you're saying? She's in the kitchen now. Perhaps we should go in, and you can complain directly to her."

Henri held up his hand to quiet the girl. "Shhhh . . . silly girl." His tone was placating. "There's no need to talk to Dominique. I was merely teasing. You can never tell when I'm teasing, can you? I was joking about the tip. My friend Picasso is tight."

"He has little money," she replied. She was tempted to add, "Since when has Picasso become your friend?"—but the look on Henri's face made her hold her tongue. For once.

"And often he has little food," Paco added. "When I helped him move into his studio at the Bateau-Lavoir, he couldn't pay me for my labor."

126

"Perhaps he felt it should have been enough for you to help a fellow *artiste*," Henri said. "You were comrades, and he should have shared."

"Henri," Brigitte interrupted. "You contradict yourself. How can you call someone tight if they have no money and little food? If that is what your comrades think, I think they are . . . foolish."

Paco quickly spoke up. "It wasn't really a matter of politics between Picasso and me, for goodness' sake. The sculptor Gargallo was leaving Paris, and he sold Picasso a bed, a chair, a mattress, a bowl, a small table also. But Gargallo's studio was in Montparnasse. And Picasso was moving into the Bateau-Lavoir, here in Montmartre—completely across the city! Picasso's friend Manolo offered me five francs to push those things in a handcart from one end of Paris to another. When we arrived at the Bateau-Lavoir, I almost collapsed! But when it came time to collect my wage, Picasso—so charming—pointed out that if he and Manolo paid me the promised five francs, it would be impossible for them to eat. So he suggested that we spend the money on groceries and all dine together."

"How delightful!" said Brigitte. "And very practical, too."

"It made sense enough to me," Paco agreed. "Picasso is delightful company, when he chooses to be, and we enjoyed our feast—share and share alike. Isn't that the way things should be? Especially among those with your political philosophy, Henri?" Paco raised an eyebrow at Henri as he awaited an answer.

"Things should be that way—but they aren't." Henri insisted. "When my work is finished, things will change. Everyone will be equal. The government will see to it."

"What about the time Paco described—with Picasso and Manolo?" said Brigitte. "They shared without a government making them do so. Everyone ate together in Picasso's studio. It was just people, sharing."

"Isn't that what your political philosophy wants?" Paco interjected. "That no one have power over anyone else? What is more equal than friends sharing a meal? If Picasso had paid me, he would have had power over me. At least, that's what you seem to be saying. As it is, we shared a meal and no one made us do so."

"I believe you must be jealous, Henri," said Brigitte teasingly. "When have you shared a meal with Picasso?"

At that comment, Henri's face drained of its color, and he set his lips in a straight line. "Do not make fun of me, Brigitte. I could share a meal with Picasso and his *bande* any time I wish. He takes me and my views quite seriously."

"Henri . . . no one is making fun of you. You are the one who takes everything so seriously. 'Your views.'

That's exactly what I mean. Your views are just that—yours. Perhaps few others share them—have you considered that?" Brigitte drew courage from the fact that Paco was standing nearby.

"Oh, others share them." Henri let the sentence hang in the air. "Believe me, Brigitte. Others share them."

"In Russia, perhaps," said Paco lightly. "Russia is full of discontent, and sooner or later they will see—"

"A revolution!" cried Henri. "Russia is ripe for political overthrow, yes! And I will be part of that new beginning!"

Brigitte laughed. Henri had not seen the beautiful portraits of Russia's imperial family in Monsieur Pavlov's office—so serene, and so powerful.

"I'm sorry, Henri," she said. "It all seems so melodramatic to me. And we live in Paris now. Surely there are few anarchists here—they're all in Russia! The French have had their revolution."

"Brigitte, lower your voice," said Paco, looking around the café. "You never know who might be listening."

"That's right, Brigitte," said Henri, smirking at the girl as he stood up. "You never know."

Paco stood also. He looked at Henri directly. "She is a child, Henri," he said quietly. "Don't involve her in whatever you are planning."

Henri turned on his heel and left the room without saying a word.

Brigitte was too embarrassed to look up. So Paco thought she was a child! A child! Her cheeks burned. She was not a child! She turned her attention to clearing the table, carefully stacking two mugs together, no more, and laying them on their sides to keep them from falling off the clearing tray. She would show him! She was definitely not a child. Soon she would be on her own—living life on her terms.

Brigitte refused to look up, and Paco addressed the back of her neck. "I'm leaving for the Bateau-Lavoir now. Picasso has finally been able to purchase enough white paint to put finishing touches on the *saltimbanque* painting—such a relief to us all! I hope to see you later. And thank you, for what you did for Anna Maria," he said quietly.

Brigitte raised her head, looking directly at him. "You're welcome, of course. I couldn't stand by and watch her get into trouble."

Paco smiled at Brigitte, his blue eyes shining. "You are a good girl," he said.

"I'm not a girl!" Brigitte exclaimed, the words tumbling out of her mouth. "I'm . . . I'm practically grown." As soon as the words left her mouth, Brigitte realized how they sounded. Frantically she tried to think of something to say to Paco that wouldn't sound childish. Just then an idea came to her.

"Paco . . . is Romero back? He must be, correct?"

Paco looked surprised. "No, he isn't. Why? Have you seen him?

"Yes, a while ago by the wood stack, talking to Henri."

"Are you sure?"

Brigitte closed her eyes, picturing the man. "Yes," she said. "I'm sure, though Henri didn't admit it when I asked. But why does Romero not go back to the circus? Is his monkey all right without him?"

"For the moment," Paco answered. "But Toulouse is a stubborn little beast and won't perform without Romero. If he doesn't earn his keep, Lars will shoot him."

"No!" An image of the monkey doffing his hat, grinning his monkey grin as coins fell into his cup, popped into Brigitte's head. Toulouse could not be killed. "Paco, it's not right! How could he shoot him?"

Paco, leaving, looked back at Brigitte. "Why should Lars treat a monkey differently than he treats the rest of us?"

⁂

Dominique called from upstairs. "Brigitte? Get Henri for me, please, and come to the kitchen. I need you to taste the soup for me. I think it needs salt. I'll be there in a moment."

"I'm here, Madame," Henri called up. He was already dipping a spoon into the pot of onion soup. He tasted the broth, looking thoughtful. "I agree, Madame. It needs a pinch more." He reached for the salt crock that sat nearby.

Dominique had already descended the stairs and was taking charge of her kitchen. "Just a minute," she said tapping Henri's forearm with her wooden spoon. "Let Brigitte taste, too."

Brigitte took a ladle and sipped some of the dark broth into her mouth, holding it there to allow the flavor to settle before she swallowed. "It tastes good, Aunt. Very rich. I think I might leave it as it is. One can always add salt, but it's impossible to take it away."

Dominique Boudoin nodded and smiled. "A wise observation," she said. "You have good instincts, Brigitte—and I think you have a café in your future."

The urge to say, "But I don't want a café in my future" rose up in Brigitte, but she held her tongue. Her aunt meant well.

Henri shrugged, but he looked angry. "I still think the soup needs salt," he said. "But it is up to you, of course. I will go back to chopping wood, as it seems that is the only work I am fit for." He left, and soon they heard the sound of his ax.

"Henri is irritable lately, and I've offended him," said Dominique, watching him out the back door.

"Until you came, I always relied on him when I was unsure of my own taste buds. Here, I will take him a little pastry. He is a handsome boy. Perhaps one day you two will run this café together. Who can tell?" Dominique allowed herself a small smile as she wrapped a tart in a twist of paper and started for the backyard.

I can tell, Brigitte thought darkly.

Chapter 17

THE SPANISH LESSON

A FEW DAYS LATER, Henri stood in the pantry of the café, staring into a small mirror on the wall. *"Buenas tardes, Señor Picasso. Buenas tardes."*

"Rrrr," he said as he rolled his tongue on the roof of his mouth. *"Tarrrrdes. Tarrrrdes."* He repeated the word over and over.

"Are you all right, Henri?" Brigitte came into the small room to pick up a stack of wiping towels.

He jumped. "I'm fine," he snapped.

"You were making a funny sound."

"If you must know, you nosy girl, I was practicing rolling my Rs. One does that when one speaks Spanish. But I forget. You're from Poland."

Henri's tone seemed to equate Poland with a

garbage heap, but Brigitte allowed the insult to roll off her. "I just didn't know you spoke Spanish, that's all," she said as she put three fresh towels on her tray and reached for an empty carafe to fill with water.

"There is much you don't know about me," Henri replied quickly, picking up his own serving tray. "I plan to address Picasso and his party in the artist's native tongue. It is a nice touch that will delight Picasso."

Brigitte stopped to think. "Why do you favor Picasso like that? If you speak Spanish to him, should you not speak Russian to Monsieur Pavlov? You haven't bothered to do that, other than a greeting and a farewell. Monsieur Pavlov is also here this afternoon, at his usual table. I will be happy to let you wait on him."

"You see to Pavlov's needs, with your special deliveries on Fridays. That's enough special treatment for him. I must see to Picasso's table," he said. "I have important things to discuss with him—things you couldn't begin to understand." He picked up his tray and went into the dining room, still rolling Rs under his breath.

At Picasso's table, Henri stopped in front of Fernande. "*Buenas tardes,*" he said.

Fernande looked bewildered. "I beg your pardon?" she said in French. "I didn't understand you."

Brigitte allowed herself a quick glance at Henri.

135

The telltale flush was in his cheeks, but she had to admire his pluck. He tried once more. *"Buenas tardes,"* he repeated.

Fernande looked helplessly at Picasso, who sat sketching in his notebook, capturing the image of a child at play in the square outside the café.

"What is he saying?" she asked in rapid French. Picasso, whose own command of French was poor, seemed irritated by the interruption to his sketching. He put his charcoal down.

"I think the boy is saying good afternoon," Max Jacob said, talking as if Henri were not standing right there. Then he looked at him. *"Buenas tar-days,"* he said. "When you speak Spanish, you should speak only correct Spanish. Your Spanish sounds like a peasant talking."

Brigitte brought a bowl of Dominique's onion soup over to Monsieur Pavlov, and was a bit surprised to see him watching the exchange over his newspaper. "Do you speak Spanish, monsieur?" she asked him quietly.

"What?" said Monsieur Pavlov, startled. "Do I . . . speak Spanish? Ah . . . yes. A bit." He composed himself. "I speak several languages, my dear. The boy seems to be struggling."

Henri concentrated on pouring wine for Picasso's table. As he reached Fernande's place, she looked at him brightly. "Let's try it together. *Buenas tar-days*," she said, looking toward Picasso to see if he approved. "Now you try it, Henri. *Buenas tar-days*."

Henri flushed. Everyone was watching, much to Brigitte's amusement—including Henri's adored Picasso. Miserably, he muttered, *"Buenas tar-days."* But he had practiced rolling his Rs so many times that he could not change his pronunciation. Picasso and his friends laughed, and Henri's cheeks grew brighter.

Fernande had moved her chair slightly when she had asked Picasso what Henri was saying, and its leg now sat in the path of Henri's foot. He stumbled over it as he tipped the pitcher, pouring red wine on Fernande's sleeve—and Picasso's sketch.

Picasso jumped to his feet and let out an expletive whose meaning was perfectly clear to anyone who heard it, whether they understood Spanish or not.

"Clumsy boy!" The words tumbled out of Apollinaire's mouth as he grabbed a napkin in an effort to save the sketch. "You pour wine over the art of a master?"

Brigitte sped to the kitchen to fetch Dominique before things got out of hand. The older woman hurried into the dining room in time to see Picasso ripping the ruined page from his sketchbook. He balled it up and threw it to the floor, cursing. Fernande was mopping the sleeve of her blouse, saying all the while that she felt certain it had been an accident. Henri stood there, frozen to the spot.

"Go to the kitchen," Dominique told Henri. "You, too," she said to Brigitte, who had come back to witness what was going to happen next.

Dominique turned to Picasso and the others. She spread her hands, palms upward, and said, "I am sorry. Henri is not usually so clumsy. The boy is not himself lately. Allow me to forgive the bill for your lunch."

Brigitte was astonished. She had never witnessed Dominique forgiving a check. Never.

A free lunch! There was a bit of grumbling—especially from Apollinaire, who muttered about "wanton destruction" and "careless half-wits"—but the generous offer had a soothing effect on everyone's mood, and Dominique followed Brigitte to the kitchen, leaving a contented, if somewhat damp, table of customers behind.

In the kitchen, Henri was pacing back and forth, back and forth.

"You will wear out your boots, Henri. Stop. Sit down," Dominique said, pulling a stool in front of the fire. Henri chose to stand.

"Suit yourself, boy," Dominique sighed, taking a seat. "That was unfortunate in there, Henri, but it's not the end of the world. You need to be more careful."

"I was careful, Madame. That stupid woman had

moved her chair while she was whispering to Picasso, making fun of my Spanish. They were all making fun of me."

As he spoke, Henri took the skin off an onion and centered it on the chopping block. He reached for a butcher knife. *Whack!* The onion fell into halves.

"Now see, you've cut through the root. That's not a good technique. You don't chop an onion in the same manner as you chop wood. You know better, Henri," said Dominique.

Henri lifted his knife again, but Dominique put her hand on his arm.

"That's enough for now," she said.

"Perhaps Brigitte should take over, then?" Henri asked, his voice dripping with sarcasm. "She seems to make no mistakes."

Brigitte busied herself sorting dried beans, not daring to look up.

"What has gotten into you these days, my boy? You take offense at everything—even those who only want to help you. Of course, why you wanted to speak to those bohemians in their own tongue is beyond me."

"I—I thought it would make a good impression on them. And you have complimented Brigitte on greeting Pavlov in his tongue; I thought I would do the same for Picasso," Henri replied defiantly. "Futhermore, I don't like being made sport of, Madame. By anyone—especially Picasso."

Dominique patted his shoulder. "So, Henri, you have fallen under the little Spaniard's spell. Just like the rest of them. What is it about him that causes those around him to behave so slavishly toward him? When he rises from the table, all rise. When he is silent, all are uncomfortable. Why does everyone seek to please him?"

Henri opened his mouth to reply, but Dominique raised a hand to silence him. She had not finished.

"And why should you care that he teases because you don't lisp when you speak his language? Do you know why some Spaniards lisp? One of their kings had a speech impediment, and he insisted that all his subjects speak the way he did. That king died generations ago, but many insist on continuing the pronunciation," she said.

"Picasso would not care about that!" exclaimed Henri. "That would be imperialist thinking—" He stopped short.

"Picasso strides around Montmartre as if he were as important as a Spanish king," Dominique said. "Listen to me, Henri. The truth is, he is just another starving artist—born in Malaga, as Fernande has said. You are far too sensitive, boy, worrying about rolling Rs and lisping Ds and whether or not Picasso has taken offense at you. Such silliness."

Dominique glanced quickly in Brigitte's direction. Satisfied that her niece was also benefiting from this lesson, she turned her attention back to Henri.

"Ahhh, your lower lip sticks out far enough for a bird to perch upon it! Stop pouting, Henri," she said. "It doesn't become you. And lest you feel too sorry for yourself, remember this—it was you who spilled the wine and you who ruined his sketch."

"But, Madame," Henri began, until Dominique held up her hand for silence.

"I have made a decision. You must apologize to Picasso. In person. It is the right thing to do, and furthermore, I don't want him or any of his friends spreading the word through Montmartre that we are not a civilized place to dine. What if Monsieur Pavlov got word that our service had become sloppy? He might choose another café."

In the corner, Brigitte stole a glance first at her aunt, who looked as if the world would end should Pavlov not come to the café. Next, she glanced at Henri, whose face had turned a dangerous shade of red. Wishing she could become invisible, Brigitte returned to inspecting the dried beans as if they were crown jewels.

Dominique untied her ever-present white apron and hung it on its hook—a certain sign that she was leaving the café for an errand. As she pulled her wool cape around her shoulders, she announced, "Enough of this. I am going to Mass. Brigitte will tell you what needs to be done in preparation for tonight's meals. I have left the menu with her."

Brigitte, still absorbed in the task of sorting the beans, sighed. This was not going to be an easy afternoon.

Chapter 18

THE FIRING

"IT SHOULDN'T TAKE YOU too long to scrape these," Brigitte said, putting a basket of carrots on the work-table. She avoided Henri's sullen stare and added, "I have to leave for a while. I'm picking up some flour at Monsieur Guimet's mill."

As soon as she left the café, Brigitte sighed with relief. Dominique's confrontation with Henri had been embarrassing for everyone. She was a bit surprised to find herself, once again, feeling sorry for the boy. She pictured him going home, telling someone about his day—and realized with a start that she still did not even know where he lived. And as for telling someone about his day, he had no family to tell. *Well, neither do I,* she thought. Unless, of course, you counted

Dominique and Georges, whom she supposed she should count. Her aunt and uncle were nice, but life with them was so . . . so regular. "Boring" was another word that came to mind. Paco—now, Paco had an exciting life. A circus *saltimbanque*, an artist's model!

Paco. An idea took hold in Brigitte's head, and she quickly calculated her time. Dominique was going to Mass. She would surely go to confession first, and that meant Brigitte had enough time to stop by the Medrano, just for a little while. . . . Perhaps Paco would be there.

❧

There were no customers waiting to buy tickets, and the ticket seller was lolling against the side of his kiosk, smoking, when Brigitte arrived. The area in front of the pink tent was empty. No street performers. No free shows. Brigitte glanced at the makeshift city that housed the performers, trying to catch a glimpse of Paco. Everything seemed quiet. A few women dangled babies from their knees or stirred pots over open fires. She could see one of the Vela sisters chatting with Miss La La. The jugglers were doing stretching exercises as the strong man stood by, entertaining them with jokes and gossip. A few stray cats wandered about, sometimes earning a quick pet or even a bit of food.

Brigitte walked over to the ticket seller. "Have you seen Paco de Suarez—the *saltimbanque*?" She could feel the flush rise in her cheeks and prayed it didn't show. The man gave her a slow appraisal up and down, taking in her plain black skirt, her white blouse. In horror, she realized she had left her apron on. I look like a scullery maid, she thought, and pulled her cloak around her more tightly.

The ticket seller picked a piece of tobacco off his tongue, made a dry spit, then smiled, revealing a mouth with few teeth left. "Your boyfriend, is he?"

"No, no," she stammered quickly. "He's a friend, that's all."

"A friend, huh? Circus people don't make friends with your kind."

"I'm not a townie . . . at least, not the kind of townie you think!" Brigitte protested. Why didn't he just tell her where Paco was?

The ticket seller laughed unpleasantly. "You're a townie all right. But it's nothing to me. Last I saw Paco, he was in the back lot. Go look for him, if you like. Watch the mud. Wouldn't want to get those nice boots dirty now, would you?"

Brigitte was conscious of her new brown boots— Dominique had insisted she needed them right before Père Noël made his visit. Now, picking her way through the mud, she wished she had worn her old ones. She heard raised voices ahead. Angry conversation. She made her way toward the sounds and came upon a knot of performers standing transfixed as they listened to another of Lars's tirades. There was the acrobat family—the mother had just had a baby. She stood by, holding the child, obviously frightened. The father stared at Lars impassively. And there was the other Vela sister, and a few clowns, looking somber.

The Bearded Lady—already in costume for the street performance—was the one at the center of all the attention. She stood in front of Lars, and her submissive posture reminded Brigitte of images of saints right before their martyrdom.

"I've told you before, you eat too much! Where do you think you are? The Palace of Versailles?" Lars's face was within inches of the woman's, and she shrank back.

"You're getting fat! Who wants to look at a fat freak?"

The Bearded Lady's face was white with fear. Lars didn't want an answer, and he didn't wait for one. Instead he let his glance sweep across the performers who had gathered to watch the scene.

"This is my circus, and what I say goes. Do all of you understand that?" he demanded. Heads nodded slowly up and down. Brigitte saw that Paco merely inclined his head to one side. Anna Maria, dry-eyed and serious, held his hand.

Lars turned back to the Bearded Lady. "Well, enough is enough." He reached out and ripped the beard off her chin with one jerk.

"Ohhhh," the woman cried. Her cheeks and chin burned bright red, and she rubbed them to quiet the pain.

"You're fired. Get out of here," he said. "I can find another freak like you anytime I want."

Still silent, the woman turned to go. A few performers, including Paco, started to follow her, but some of the others drew back, as if her condition were somehow catching. Brigitte remembered the Bearded Lady's friendly wave on her first night at the circus, and how happy that gesture had made her feel. She started forward. Perhaps there was some way she could help. But the Bearded Lady, sobbing, broke away from the other performers and ran through the mud, disappearing into a tent.

Lars was still holding the beard. His eyes fell on Brigitte. "What have we here?" he said, leering. "Would you like to be my new Bearded Lady?" He twirled the nasty piece of fur in his hand, and Brigitte shook her head.

"Brigitte is my friend—" began Anna Maria, then snapped her mouth shut.

Lars looked at her. "Then perhaps she can take your place, missy. That arm is taking too long to heal."

"Oh, she was merely teasing," Brigitte protested. "I couldn't take her place. . . ." But then, for a wild moment, Brigitte thought, *Maybe I* could *join the circus! True, there were these dark moments, but there were also the parades, the music, the performers, the animals. . . .*

As if he could read her mind, Lars looked at Paco. "Bring me that monkey. It's time I got rid of it, too."

"Actually, I've had a little luck with the monkey, sir," Paco replied. He reached into a concealed pocket and pulled out a few coins which he placed in Lars's outstretched hands. "Here."

"It's not much."

"There will be more when he gets used to me," Paco replied.

Brigitte was astonished. This was the first time she had heard of Paco working with Toulouse. She waited until Lars had closed his fingers around the coins and stalked off before turning to Paco to say, "You haven't been working with Toulouse, have you? You told me he won't work with anyone but Romero."

Paco forced a slight smile. "Aren't you the clever one?" he said gently. "No, those were my wages. I was just buying Toulouse a little more time. Maybe we can find Romero."

"That may be quite a job," said a familiar voice.

Henri? What was he doing here? Brigitte spun around and faced him.

"I've peeled the carrots, in case you're wondering," Henri said. "I assume you have picked up the flour?" Henri held an apple and was paring off slices with the bone-handled knife.

"And you've brought Dominique's good knife with you?" Brigitte said, deftly changing the subject.

Henri waved it in the air. "Oh, this? I was taking it to the tinker, to have it sharpened." He swallowed the last of the apple and turned to Paco. "Brigitte may have told you, *saltimbanque,* but I am to apologize to Picasso. On orders from Dominique."

Paco looked amused. "What crime have you committed, Henri?"

"I spilled a bit of wine—by accident, mind you—on one of his sketches, and he screamed like a stuck pig."

"He has a short temper—especially when it comes to his art," Paco replied.

"It was a mere sketch. He produces dozens of them in a week. So tell me, this masterpiece of his, the one that you pose for—is it finished?"

"Almost. He has finally come up with some white paint, so now he finishes. The canvas is huge, but a few more strokes for the clouds, and it will be complete."

"Fine. Fine. Just tell me, which studio is his? I want to get in, apologize, and get out. I thought I could save myself some steps if I came here to ask directions from you."

Paco seized on an unexpected opportunity. "It seems I have information you want, Henri. What are you willing to pay for it?"

"Now see here, *saltimbanque* . . ."

"No, you see, Henri. I must find Romero. He has to make a choice. Return to the circus and go back to work, or return to the circus to take Toulouse away with him. But he must return. If you had seen what just happened here . . . The circus people are sick of Lars and his cruelty—to us, as well as the animals. If Lars shoots that monkey, there will be chaos, and many people could get hurt."

"So? People get hurt all the time," Henri replied.

"It would be nice if we could prevent it from time to time." Paco's tone was cold. "Anna Maria, take Brigitte with you. I need to talk to Henri alone."

There it was again. Dismissal, as if she were somehow on Anna Maria's level—a child.

"Come on, Brigitte," Anna Maria said. "Watch me practice on the Spanish web. I've got to get my arm stronger." Anna Maria lowered her voice. "I'll show you how it's done."

Although she was eager to see how the Spanish web was performed, as they walked toward the tent Brigitte said, "I don't have much time. Dominique will be looking for me soon."

Anna Maria was excited, full of chatter. "Maybe

you can come back again tomorrow. I'll show you some today. And then you can come back tomorrow! Wouldn't it be good if you could do my act until I get better?" She looked up at Brigitte, eyes shining. "Wouldn't that be good?"

The idea hit Brigitte with the force of lightning. Could she possibly substitute for Anna Maria? Even Lars had hinted it could happen. "Well . . ." Brigitte began, trying to hide the excitement in her voice. "Well, that might be good."

Chapter 19

THE TRAPEZE

BRIGITTE HAD HAD JUST ENOUGH TIME to practice a few simple turns on the Spanish web before needing to return to the café, but the experience was enough to rob her of sleep that night. Anna Maria's suggestion kept echoing over and over in her head. *Wouldn't it be good if you could do my act until I get better?*

Perhaps she could take Anna Maria's place—just long enough for her arm to heal. And then—well, by then, she would have perfected the skills she needed to work on the trapeze. And once she perfected the trapeze and could fly across the tent, sequins glistening, she would be a star. And Lars would offer her a permanent job. And he would never fire her. She would show him how good she could be. Why, she would be just like Miss La La—his favorite. The thoughts roiled and boiled in her head like the lentils bubbling in Dominique's soup. However, the following afternoon, when an unexpected errand allowed her to slip away to the Medrano once again, her nighttime fantasies were tempered by daytime reality.

At Brigitte's request, Anna Maria had managed to cobble together some kind of costume from odds and ends of circus clothing. Brigitte found herself dressed in a pair of black leggings that were a bit too large and a wrinkled red satin blouse that fell to her knees, tied at the waist with a once-sequined belt. Anna Maria had insisted she pin her braid up—for safety—and now Brigitte stood on the small training platform, midway between the sawdust of the ring and the top of the tent.

"Stand with your legs far apart. Good. Now, put your hips forward, and keep your shoulders back, just like I showed you," Anna Maria called up to her.

Brigitte drew in a shaky breath, trying not to look down. She had definitely preferred yesterday's practice, wrapping herself in the Spanish web, slowly turning round and round.

Just then, a voice cut through the silence in the tent. "What are you doing?" It was Paco, looking first at his sister, then up at Brigitte.

"Nothing," said Anna Maria, almost choking on the word.

"Nothing? I leave for a while, and when I return, look what happens. Now you're into more mischief, putting Brigitte up on the trapeze. Wasn't yesterday enough? You showed her the Spanish web."

"Don't be angry at her, Paco," Brigitte called down. "It's my fault. I begged her to let me try. When I arrived today, they had taken down the Spanish web, so I climbed up here. I've always wanted to try the trapeze. I can do this."

Paco shook his head, looking worried. "It's not as simple as it looks, Brigitte. You should have waited." He sighed deeply. "We have to get you down before Lars sees you. You want to fly? Then lift the bar and push off the platform."

Brigitte had not felt frightened until that moment. Suddenly Paco and Anna Maria seemed far smaller than they should, and the sawdust in the center ring was a long, long way down. At least there was a safety net, but the idea of landing in it was even more frightening. Anna Maria had shown what could happen, and she stood below, her injured arm still hanging by her side at an awkward angle. What would Dominique say if she returned to the café with an arm that no longer worked? She called down to Paco, "Wait. I'm not ready!"

"Is that so? Well, you should have considered that before you climbed up there." Then, seeing her white face, he softened. "You'll be all right. There's a net. Nothing can happen. Unless, of course, you want to come down the way you went up—using the rigging steps."

Climbing up had not been easy, but Brigitte would have died before she admitted that fact. The idea of going down those unstable steps—defeated—held no appeal either.

"No. I'm going to fly. I'm going to do it."

"As you please," he said. "Now do as I say. Lift the bar and push off."

Anna Maria cheered her on. "You can do it, Brigitte! I know you can do it. Is there some rosin up there? Put it on your hands."

"I've already done that. They're still sweaty. What if I drop the bar?"

"You'll fall into the net, that's all. Try to land on your back. Now do it. Do it quickly, before anyone sees us," said Paco, looking around to be certain that Lars was nowhere in sight.

It was now or never. Brigitte held her breath and closed her eyes. From the ground, the trapeze had looked simple. From this height, it was another matter. Brigitte drew in her breath, lifted the bar and pushed off the platform. Once airborne, she felt a rush of excitement and exhilaration as she swung across the center ring. The exhilaration disappeared quickly, however, when her arms began to burn with the effort of holding onto the slender bar.

Standing below, Paco could see her starting to struggle. "Just drop the bar, relax, and fall into the net. Remember—try to land on your back, if you can," he called up to her.

Brigitte's fingers felt as if they had been welded to the trapeze. She thought, *Let go! Let go!* But her fingers would not let go. Her strength was failing, and she no longer had the energy to pump the trapeze into an arc that would return her to the safety of the platform and a descent via the rigging steps.

At last, with great effort, she forced her aching fingers open, then let out a scream as she felt them lose their grip on the trapeze bar, and she began her tumble into the net below.

It was a hard landing, and it hurt. The net's rough webbing scraped her cheek, and for a moment she lay on her stomach, motionless, checking for sharp pains that could indicate a broken bone or a dislocated shoulder. She wanted to cry, but not even Miss La La's wild horse would have dragged tears out of her eyes in front of Paco.

Anna Maria hurried over. "Are you all right?"

Brigitte managed to roll over and sit up. "I think so," she said.

Anna Maria started to applaud, but stopped as

pain burst through her shoulder. "You were very brave, Brigitte," she said. "I know it can be frightening up there."

Paco offered her his hand. "That wasn't bad for a townie. Let me help you off the net."

Brigitte felt a wash of happiness at his approval. Within a minute she was standing on the sawdust. "It was good for my first time, wasn't it?" she said.

"Your first time, and your last," Paco said briskly.

"What? Paco, let me go up again. Please. I—I loved it." The words stuck in her throat. She hadn't loved it, but maybe it would grow on her, who could say? At least it was exciting—much more so than running the café.

"Hurry," Paco said, stopping her fantasy. "We can't take a chance on Lars seeing us. We don't let outsiders into the circus."

"Well, you let Picasso in," Brigitte said, stumbling after him and Anna Maria, one end of her sequined belt dragging in the sawdust. "He and Apollinaire, and Fernande—they all come and they go as they please. I've seen them talking to the performers. You even said Picasso painted himself into that masterpiece he just finished—as a harlequin. And he made Apollinaire a jester. You told me so! They want to be part of the circus, and so do I." She knew she sounded like the child she was so often accused of being, but she didn't care and couldn't help herself.

"I said he paints himself that way. I didn't say he is a harlequin, did I?" said Paco, hurrying them out of the tent. "Picasso is an artist, and you are—"

"I know—a townie, and a child, and a waitress!" Brigitte was ready to cry, and she fought back hot tears. "Who wants to be a waitress in a café, working all day long, washing and peeling vegetables, scrubbing tables, folding linens, smelling like cabbages and onions?"

"I think it would be nice," said Anna Maria timidly. "You would have food to eat, as much as you want. And you would stay in one place all the time. And you wouldn't get hurt, like I did."

"You can get hurt in a café, too, Anna Maria," Brigitte answered. "There are plenty of sharp knives, and pots of boiling water. Look at my hand." Brigitte pointed to the nasty scar that ran across the fleshy part of her palm, beneath her right thumb. The remains of the trapeze rosin made it stand out even more. "That came from one of Aunt Dominique's carving knives."

Anna Maria inspected the scar, running a dirty finger over the raised white line, then took Brigitte's hand into her own.

"But people don't come to the café hoping to see you get cut or thinking you might burn yourself! Those are accidents. A lot of people come to the circus just to see if we'll get hurt. That's what Lars says. They want excitement, and Lars says we have to give it to them—

or we'll be fired. Isn't that right, Paco?" Anna Maria's hand moved up her injured arm, and she began to massage the ache in it.

Suddenly a commotion broke out by the door to the rough wooden shack that served as the manager's office. Clowns mingled with ticket collectors, animal trainers with acrobats, all buzzing together like angry bees.

"Anna Maria, take Brigitte back to change her clothes. I'll find out what's going on."

"Wait, I want to come!" cried Brigitte.

"Brigitte! If Lars sees you in that silly costume—you shouldn't be here!" Paco said, exasperated. "Do you want us to lose our jobs?"

"No," she whispered.

"Come on, Brigitte." Anna Maria took Brigitte back to the costume tent, where earlier, the girls had raided a trunk for Brigitte's clothing. Brigitte was happy to exchange the sweat-scented circus clothes for the plain but clean skirt and blouse she wore at the café. When she was dressed, the two girls went to find Paco.

"What's happening, Paco?" Anna Maria asked. "Have they . . . has Lars . . . hurt the monkey?" She could not bring herself to say the word "shot."

Paco shook his head. "No. Toulouse is still alive. Lars has cut the wages again. He says the crowd is thin, and the profits aren't there. He's threatening to cut some acts, too, so everyone is furious."

"Can he do that?" asked Brigitte. "Can he just cut out acts and send people away?"

"He's the director of the circus. He can do whatever he wants," Paco answered shortly. "Anna Maria, you go back to our tent. Be with Mother and Manuel. I'm going to take Brigitte home."

Chapter 20

THE WALK HOME

Winter was upon them, and Brigitte shivered beneath her wool cloak. She looked at Paco. His *saltimbanque* costume was so thin, and he had no coat.

"Aren't you freezing?" she said.

"I'm used to it," he said simply, and he took her elbow as they picked their way carefully over the ruts in the dirt street.

Brigitte pulled her cloak around her more tightly, and in doing so, she felt the nuts in her pocket. She pulled them out and handed them to Paco. "Will you give these to Toulouse?" she asked. "I meant to do it myself, but I . . . well, I got involved with the trapeze."

Paco took the almonds from her hand. "I will, if Toulouse hasn't been roasted for dinner."

"Paco!" Brigitte was horrified. "You said he was alive!"

The boy relented. "I am joking," he admitted. "But it is true that without his master, Toulouse is doomed. The stupid animal will not work with anyone else."

"If I were part of the circus, he would work with me," Brigitte said. As soon as the words were out of her mouth, she saw herself dressed in a glittering costume, grinding the barrel organ, singing to the crowds who would flock to throw coins in the monkey's little cup. Her heart lifted. There were other ways to be part of the circus than flying through the air.

Paco interrupted her reverie. "The circus isn't a life for you, Brigitte."

"It could be. I can do it," she protested stubbornly.

"Perhaps you can. But why would you? There are too many risks, too much deprivation. You would never fit in."

"What do you know? I could fit in. I could!" Brigitte could feel her cheeks burning in the cold air. Had she not already proved her courage on the trapeze?

"And do you want to disappear like Romero?"

Brigitte laid a hand on Paco's arm to pull him back; he had been two steps ahead of her.

"Have you learned anything?"

"I talked to Henri," Paco seemed to hesitate, reluctant to continue.

"You did? What did he say? It was Romero Henri was talking to that day! I tell you, it was!"

"I know. I believe you." They walked, together this time, in silence. Finally Paco sighed, assessing his words carefully. "Brigitte, if I share this information with you, you must give me your word that it remains with you, and you only. No telling your aunt—or Anna Maria. Do I have your promise?"

"Oh, I promise!" Brigitte had no intention of talking to her aunt about Paco de Suarez in anything but the most impersonal way.

Paco hesitated a moment longer, considering his words. "Do you remember when Henri wanted directions to Picasso's studio?"

Brigitte nodded, also remembering that she had been dismissed from the conversation like a small child.

"Henri was full of questions for me, and I traded information for information. He wanted to know all details of Picasso's studio—exactly what floor of the Bateau-Lavoir it occupied, how it was laid out, everything I could think of. I can't imagine why that information was important to him, but it seemed to be. In return, I wanted to know what happened to Romero."

"So did you find out?" Brigitte was already imagining the homecoming scene with Toulouse.

"Not exactly. But Henri did tell me that Romero is more than a simple organ grinder."

"He is?" Brigitte was fascinated.

Abruptly, Paco changed subjects. "Brigitte, what does Monsieur Pavlov do?"

"I don't know," Brigitte answered impatiently. What did Monsieur Pavlov have to do with this? "He's a diplomat. He works at the Russian consulate."

Paco stopped walking and glanced around the street. When he seemed satisfied that they would not be overheard, he looked at Brigitte solemnly and spoke quietly and deliberately. "Brigitte, the consulate is where the offices of the Okhrana—the Russian secret police—are located."

"Don't be silly, Paco," Brigitte burst out. "I've been there. It's a consulate, for goodness' sake. And anyway, if it houses the secret police, how come it isn't a secret?"

"Shhhhh!" Paco said, looking around again to be certain no one was nearby. "Most of the Russians in Paris know about Okhrana—especially the ones in the circus, who have fled from the tsar's oppression. Henri . . ."

Before he could finish his thought, Brigitte interrupted. "Henri is Russian! His real name is Adrik—did you know that?"

When Paco shook his head, Brigitte continued. "Henri told me about his father . . . how he cooked for a circus, and how the circus manager fired him. For no good reason. Henri seemed very bitter. I think that's why he speaks so—" Brigitte faltered, thinking of a way to describe Henri's attitude toward the circus, "—dismissively of . . . of the Medrano."

"Henri is more familiar with the Medrano than you may think," Paco said.

"Well, he knows about circus life, of course," Brigitte answered quickly.

"He was once part of it," Paco said simply.

"Henri? Performing in a circus?" Brigitte could barely hide her astonishment.

"I didn't say he performed," Paco said. "I said he was once a part of the circus family."

"Well yes, I've said as much. Back in Russia."

"And in Paris, too," Paco said. "It seems Henri and his father wound up at the Medrano, because Henri's father had a friend there."

"Romero?" It was a guess, but Brigitte knew she was right.

Paco nodded. "Yes. Romero got Henri's father a job, cooking for the Medrano. But the father was only there a short while before he disappeared. It was well over a year ago, and frankly, I paid little attention at the time. People are always coming and going at a circus, and the Russians stick to themselves. One day, when Romero was going for a stroll in Montmartre, he saw the sign for help hanging outside Dominique's café and he told Henri—urged Henri, really—to take it. *Voilà!* Henri got the job."

"Why did Romero want Henri to leave the circus?"

"I suspect Romero didn't want Henri to have the same fate as his father before him."

"To be an itinerant cook?"

"To disappear without a trace," Paco corrected.

Brigitte nodded, pieces of the puzzle falling into place. "So that is how Henri knows Romero—Romero was a friend of his father's. Henri never told me that."

"It seems as if Henri wants to keep his connection to Romero to himself," Paco said. "Of course, he knows that I knew something . . . I was at the Medrano when Henri and his father first arrived." Paco said.

"If Romero is more than an organ grinder, did Henri tell you what else he does? Or did—before he disappeared?"

Paco shook his head. "I know nothing more with certainty, but I am putting things together from common gossip around the tents and a few things Henri said." Paco looked closely at Brigitte. "Are you certain you know nothing more about Monsieur Pavlov?"

Brigitte racked her brain. "Well, one day Monsieur Pavlov told me about the tsar and his family. He explained something about every single portrait that hung in the consulate's entrance hall. It was almost as if they were members of his own family. He adores them."

Paco listened attentively. "Pavlov must be quite high up in the organization," he said, his eyebrows rising at the thought. "Brigitte, Okhrana is ruthless. They murder people in cold blood. At the least, they deport those whom they think are plotting against the tsar. They disappear without a trace. Often to labor camps in Siberia."

"Do you think this happened to Henri's father?" Brigitte shivered at the thought of Siberia. Even at Saint Stanislaus, there was some talk about the Russian labor camps in the desolate northernmost parts of the Russian empire. Still, Siberia had seemed so remote. . . . Brigitte wished she had paid more attention in class. "But this is Paris! Not Moscow or St. Petersburg!"

"The Okhrana are all over Paris, watching for people who might cause problems for them. Their enemies just . . . disappear."

"Their enemies," said Brigitte. "Like Romero?"

"Like Romero," agreed Paco. "I don't know what he was up to, but Henri does. And he knows that Monsieur Pavlov knows all about it."

"Is that what happened to Henri's father?"

"Probably. Henri didn't say, but it makes sense."

"But can't the French police interfere? If we went to them and said that we thought the Russians had taken Romero, wouldn't they—"

"The French police are not going to listen to the words of a *saltimbanque*—and a Spanish one, to boot. And anyone—everyone—says the Sûreté Générale cooperate with the Okhrana. They don't want anoth-er revolution here," Paco said heavily.

Brigitte was thinking. "That must be why Henri thought of delivering Monsieur Pavlov's food on Fridays," she said. "He wanted to find out about the secret police . . ."

". . . or what happened to his father. And he didn't count on your charm winning over Monsieur Pavlov."

Brigitte's mind was whirling. Was this why Henri seemed to resent her so? Had her deliveries interfered with his plans to find his father? She still had a hard time imagining the suave Monsieur Pavlov as anything but a diplomat. But the story was making sense. Poor Henri! He had lost his mother, his father, and now his friend Romero. . . .

"Paco," she said. "Henri is always so interested in Picasso, always trying to start up a friendship. Why is that, do you suppose? Could it have anything to do with this? Uncle Georges once said the police were interested in some of our customers . . . he could have meant Picasso." Brigitte paused for a moment, consid-ering what she had just said. "Of course, Henri is quite angry with Picasso at the moment, so friendship is far from his mind."

"Correct. At the moment Henri's thoughts are taken up with how to make an apology he resents having to offer." Paco shook his head, trying to make his thoughts fall into place. "It's late. We need to rest. Perhaps tomorrow will bring more clarity to our thoughts." They had reached the square in front of the Café Dominique.

"I know!" said Brigitte. "I deliver food to Monsieur Pavlov tomorrow. I'll simply ask him some questions . . ."

"No!" said Paco, turning to face her. "Do you want to disappear like Romero? Brigitte, think! Is Pavlov going to say, 'Oh yes, sit down, my dear and let me tell you all that is going on with the secret police. I have Romero right here. You can have him back now. I didn't realize that his monkey needed him.' "

Brigitte blushed furiously.

"Promise me that you will not speak to Monsieur Pavlov. Give the food to the maid when you deliver it, and turn around and go home."

"I promise that I will not ask Monsieur Pavlov about Romero," said Brigitte, choosing her words with precision.

"Good. Now look what I have for you—a ticket to the circus. The ticket seller had saved it for his brother, but he cannot come. It's yours, if you want it."

"Oh, Paco! Of course I want it! Thank you!" Brigitte said, taking the ticket. She paused, studying the little piece of pasteboard. "It's for tomorrow night."

"Yes. Is there a problem?"

"No . . . I don't think so. I have to deliver an

evening meal to Monsieur Pavlov tomorrow. Aunt Dominique says he is entertaining some people from Russia." Brigitte calculated the time it would take her to serve the meal and get to the circus. "But he wants to dine early, so I should have enough time. I'll see you tomorrow night. Will you meet me after the show?"

"Yes. Wait by the center ring."

They were at the café. Suddenly happy, Brigitte pushed the door open and stepped in.

"Good night!" she called to Paco, and watched as he walked away, his costume becoming a blur of colors—rose and blue.

Chapter 21

THE LETTER

THE FOLLOWING MORNING Brigitte woke from a fitful sleep, rose, and poured water from her pitcher into the basin that sat on top of the chest of drawers. As she splashed the cold water on her face, conflicting thoughts about Monsieur Pavlov flapped back and forth in her mind—one way, and then another, like clothes whipped on a clothesline.

How could he be anything but a simple diplomat? How could he be part of the ruthless secret police? He was so courtly, so distinguished. But still, Paco would not lie to her. But then, what was it Apollinaire had written about the *saltimbanques*? "Cunning, dexterous, poverty-stricken—and lying"? Brigitte shook the thought out of her head. Perhaps it is Henri who is lying to Paco. . . . She patted her face dry.

She had promised Paco there would be no questions about Romero when she made her delivery. But that did not mean she couldn't take a good look around at the Russian consulate. And she could still ask Monsieur Pavlov questions about anything except Romero, couldn't she?

Brigitte's spirits soared. Paco would be so proud of her! He had said she didn't know how to take the kinds of risks that circus life presented. She would show him! She could take a risk! Soaring on a trapeze was one thing. Spying was another. *I can do this*, she told herself again.

"Brigitte!"

"Coming, Aunt Dominique!" she called.

<hr />

Later that afternoon, when the lunch business had died away, Brigitte came into the kitchen and saw Dominique eyeing the remains of a roast of beef that sat on the counter.

"Ah, Brigitte," she said as soon as the girl came into the room. "Have you seen my favorite carving knife? The one with the handle made of ram's horn? I've searched all over for it."

Brigitte glanced at the wooden block where her aunt stored her knives. "Oh . . . I remember. Henri took it to the tinker. He said it needed sharpening."

"I don't know what's gotten into that boy," Dominique said. "I had that knife sharpened two weeks ago. I will certainly have a word with him when he gets here. He is late again." Dominique started cutting slices from the slab of beef.

"*Alors!* If I just had my good knife! Monsieur Pavlov has asked for *rosbif au jus*. The slices should be thin, delicate. This knife saws through the meat," said Dominique, looking at the pieces of beef with dismay as she arranged them on a deep platter. "Perhaps I can use the drippings to cover the ugliness of these slices."

She sighed. "This is not as tempting as it should be." She covered the platter with a clean towel and set it in the bottom of the delivery basket. Next she picked three thin baguettes of bread from the stack she had baked earlier in the day as well as a jar of her own pickles.

"This is nothing more than a picnic," she said, worried. "I wonder if Monsieur Pavlov is tiring of my *coq au vin?* I think I'll add some sweets." Dominique crossed to the pie safe in the kitchen and returned with six lemon tarts, which she added to the basket.

"If you add much more, I'm not going to be able to carry it all, Aunt," said Brigitte. "It's just Monsieur Pavlov and a few others, isn't it?"

"Actually, he said more diplomats had come to town, and he thought a picnic such as this would be easier to serve. But I could have fixed enough *cassoulet* or *coq au vin* to feed an army, if need be," said Dominique, who never wanted anyone to think she could not rise to a feeding challenge.

The clock on the wall chimed five times. "Ahhhh! You must hurry, child. I promised him the food would arrive by five thirty."

Brigitte slid her arm under the handle of the basket and set out for the offices on the Rue de Grenelle. As she walked, Brigitte thought about her plan—then realized she had none. She had not let her imagination carry her beyond her conviction that she could discover something about Romero at Monsieur Pavlov's townhouse, but she had no idea how she could make that happen. She had never been further inside than the entrance hall, and that only once—the day Monsieur Pavlov had talked about the portraits of the tsars so glowingly.

She hurried. Aunt Dominique would not want her to be late—and she wanted to get there, too, to see the consulate with new eyes. Very soon she had arrived on the stoop of number 97 Rue de Grenelle. Brigitte set down the heavy basket and knocked with the brass doorknocker.

A maid, younger than the usual housekeeper, opened the door and gestured Brigitte inside. "Put the things in that office," she said, gesturing to the one at the left of the entryway. "I'll go get the money for you."

Brigitte walked into the office and placed her basket on top of a cabinet that sat behind a desk. She waited. The silence of the house fell around her, and Brigitte strained her ears, willing them to hear something—anything—that would provide a clue to Romero. The clock in the hall struck once, indicating five thirty.

Brigitte's heart was pounding in her throat. She was alone in this office. Perhaps something in a trash can would give her a clue. She walked a few steps to peer into the one by the desk. It was empty. An efficient maid. *Aunt Dominique would be proud of her,* Brigitte thought.

The house remained silent. Brigitte looked around the room. Nothing lay exposed; any information was safely tucked into drawers or cabinets. The efficient maid would be back any minute with the money. Brigitte began to unpack the contents of her basket, arranging the items carefully on top of the cabinet. "You eat with your eyes as well as your mouth," Dominique often said.

Footsteps behind her made Brigitte jump. "Here is the money for the meal," said the maid. "Will you be much longer? I need to leave."

"No . . . it will only take a few minutes more to get everything ready," Brigitte answered. An idea popped into her head. "I'll let myself out," she offered helpfully.

The maid, eager to be on her way, nodded and disappeared from the room. Brigitte thought quickly. She scooped up the money, then walked quietly across the office and peered into the entrance hall. There was still no one in sight. She went to the front door, opened it, and slammed it shut. Then she quickly slipped off her shoes and, silent as a cat, ran into the office across from the room where she had laid out the food. There were heavy velvet drapes on the windows, and it was easy to conceal herself among their folds.

As she had hoped, within five minutes the maid appeared in the entrance hall, her cloak over her arm. From her hiding place, Brigitte saw the young girl look into the room where the picnic was displayed. The maid walked over, inspected the food, and took several samples of the *rosbif au jus*, licking the jus from her fingers between pieces. Dominique would have had a fit, Brigitte thought.

Satisfied, the maid headed to the front door, where she took a brass key from a fob hanging at her waist and locked it. Then she disappeared toward the back of the house. A few minutes later, Brigitte heard another door close. Cautiously, she peered out the window from behind the drapery and saw the maid walking jauntily down the street. She was gone.

Brigitte remained hidden for another minute or so, listening. Her heart pounded in her chest so heavily that she felt certain someone standing near her would have been able to hear it. Monsieur Pavlov would come for his dinner soon, and he would probably bring the others with him. Anything she was going to do, she needed to do now.

Brigitte moved from her hiding place and edged toward the large desk in the center of the room. Carefully she slid open its center drawer. Inside there were pencils, a pen, a blotter for the ink, and some stationery. Nothing remarkable at all.

Brigitte pushed the drawer closed, and wood scraping against wood suddenly produced a loud squeaking sound. Her heart leaped in her chest, and she stood absolutely still. The house remained silent. After a moment, she straightened the drawer on its runners. As she did so, she noticed her palms sweating as much as they had on the trapeze. Where was Monsieur Pavlov? Was he in the house? Could he hear her?

The two drawers on either side of the desk were next. One contained office supplies—envelopes and a box of unsharpened pencils; some extra jars of ink. The other drawer was set up in files, but the headings on each were written in Russian, as were the reports inside. Some were sealed with red wax. They looked important, but Brigitte could not summon the courage to break the wax seals—and besides, she couldn't read Russian; she just spoke a few phrases. Then she saw something at the back that pricked her interest. The file was simply titled Montmartre, and it did not have a diplomatic seal. Her hands were shaking as she pulled it from its place and opened it.

On top, there was a letter from Monsieur Pavlov to someone in the French Sûreté Générale—the police. "Copy" and "Confidential" had been scrawled across its top in red pencil. The letter was written in French.

February 16, 1905
Dear Capitaine LeMaistre:

Information has come to my attention about the people whose names follow in this report. Through our investigations, we have reason to believe these persons may have firsthand knowledge of a plot to assassinate Nicholas II. The unfortunate events of January 22 immediately past do nothing to allay our fears.

I shall continue my visits to the Café Dominique and shall continue to keep all parties under my surveillance. When the time comes, I will, as usual, appreciate the cooperation of the French government police in removing this threat to our governments' national security. Anarchists and revolutionaries must be purged from our midst in any manner possible. The names of offenders are listed below. However, I am certain there are more people acting and active in Montmartre.

1. Monsieur Henri Burtsev, Russian name: Adrik Burtsev
His father was an émigré from Russia after the first purge. Father
is in labor camp in Siberia. Young Burtsev is employed at Café
Dominique. Is a low-level operative, but passionate for his cause
and is linked to others in the revolutionary chain. He has led us
to our most important suspect, Vaclav Romero.

The paper shook in Brigitte's trembling hands.

2. Vaclav Romero works at the Cirque Medrano, begging
coins using a monkey as bait. Romero definitely assisted with the
planning of the peasant uprising known as Bloody Sunday that
took place on January 22 of this year. We have solid informa-
tion that Romero is now deeply involved plotting an assassina-
tion attempt on Nicholas II. His capture is certain. Once it is
done, we will rely on the Sûreté Générale to facilitate his depor-
tation to Siberia, until we can decide his ultimate fate.

Brigitte could feel tiny beads of perspiration pop
out on her upper lip. Paco was right. Monsieur Pavlov
was not the genteel diplomat he had seemed. She read
on, quickly.

3. Pablo Picasso, an artist whose studio is on Rue Ravignan.
He is a frequent visitor to the café where Burtsev is employed, and
goes there with a group of his friends, all artists and writers with
suspicious political inclinations. Picasso himself is a Spanish

national, though he claims to be Catalan as well. I have him under personal surveillance at this time. I suspect Burtsev is actively trying to recruit him for the revolutionary cause.

Picasso! No wonder Henri was always hovering around him—he thought Picasso was an anarchist! So Henri was hoping to get Picasso to join him and his comrades. If she had not been in so much danger, Brigitte would have laughed out loud. Picasso might talk revolution, but as Aunt Dominique often said, the only revolution he was really interested in was one started by his art. This must be why Monsieur Pavlov was always at the café—he was watching Picasso and his "suspicious" friends! And poor Aunt Dominique thought it was her cooking!

I trust you to treat this information with the greatest confidentiality, until we are ready to act jointly.

I remain, gentlemen, at your service,

Vladimir Pavlov
Deputy Director, Okhrana

Carefully Brigitte placed the letter back into its file and slid the desk drawer closed. Despite the brave talk of the night before, now that she knew what was happening, all she really wanted to do was leave. She wanted to run. No, she wanted to race—all the way back to the warmth and safety of the Café Dominique, and her generous, sharp aunt, and the *coq au vin*, and the napkins needing to be washed and folded, and even the onions waiting to be sliced for the soup.

Quickly Brigitte pulled her shoes on and went to the front door—but as soon as she placed her hand on the knob, she remembered the maid locking it. She tried anyway, wishing that something magical would happen and the door would open without a key. But it remained locked.

Brigitte set out to find the servants' door, the one the maid had used when she left the house. She moved carefully, alert for Monsieur Pavlov or another member of the secret police. Where was everyone? Darting from one doorway to the next, she found the back entrance—but that door, too, was locked.

Brigitte was trapped.

Chapter 22

THE ESCAPE

BRIGITTE WAS NOW on the second floor, carefully peering out windows, looking for ways to escape.

A commotion outside in the courtyard by the carriage house sent her back to the window that overlooked it. The scene in the courtyard below made her stomach lurch. Pavlov was outside, with five other men—and Romero, whose hands were tied behind his back.

There was a light on in the carriage house. So that's where Pavlov and the rest of the "diplomats" had been! She opened the casement, just a bit.

"You know you must talk eventually, Romero," said Pavlov, his voice loud and rough.

Romero's head was bowed, and he shook his head.

Pavlov tried again. "We know who your friends are."

Again, the man who played the barrel organ shook his head.

Two men grabbed Romero by his shirt and roughly hustled him back to the carriage house. Within minutes, the doors opened and a black carriage, its shades pulled down, rumbled out of the courtyard and headed into the streets of Paris. Brigitte watched as Pavlov and three others walked inside the consulate.

Brigitte thought of Toulouse and hot tears stung her eyes. The monkey—and Romero—were doomed. She drew back from the window, afraid the men would see her, and she would be next.

Brigitte sat down to think. How long would she be trapped here? She had already missed meeting Paco at the circus. Her aunt knew she was going to the circus this night, but still, Dominique would be expecting her to come home after the performance. She would be frantic if Brigitte didn't return to the café at a reasonable time. What time was it? *Maybe she'll come for me!* Brigitte thought, then realized her aunt had no idea she was there. If Dominique set out on a search, it would be to the circus, not here. And if Dominique eventually came here—Brigitte swallowed hard. It could be too late.

At the thought of the café, Brigitte felt a rush of feeling that could only be called homesickness. With a start, she realized that life at the café made her feel safe. Even loved. Dominique's rules were clear and—for the most part, Brigitte admitted to herself—fair. As long as she lived within them, Brigitte was free to do as she pleased. Tears formed in the corners of her eyes and threatened to spill down her cheeks. She was not free now.

She moved across the hallway to another window that looked down on the Rue de Grenelle. She opened the drapes slightly, and below her, she saw movement. Someone had darted into the bushes. Pavlov was inside. She was certain of that. She stared for another moment, then moved back from the window.

Ping! Something hit the pane, but Brigitte could not bring herself to move or to hope.

A second *ping!* What was it? Cautiously Brigitte peered outside. Paco moved into the yellow circle of light that the lamp cast on the street.

When Brigitte saw him, her mouth fell open in astonishment. She moved into the full window, allowing him to see her.

Paco waved his arms. "Come down!" he mimed. She shook her head and pointed to the window sash. The tall window was unlocked, but like all the others, it was a casement window, and it cranked open just enough to let in air. She put her face against the opening and spoke as loudly as she dared.

"I'm locked in! I can't get out! And Pavlov's here. Downstairs."

"The roof?" Paco exaggerated his lips and pointed upward. "Find a way to the roof!"

Brigitte shrugged and put up her hands, shaking her head.

Paco held up four fingers, one at a time. "First floor, second floor, third floor, attic." He wiggled the last finger.

Brigitte grasped what he was trying to say and disappeared from the window. Quietly she began to search all the closets on the top floor of the building, acutely aware of the men eating and talking downstairs. On the fifth try, she was lucky. The door opened onto a staircase that led to the attic, and in the attic there was a window. It was only locked from the inside, and Brigitte opened it easily and stepped out onto the flat roof. Paco stood below.

"I'm here," she said. As she looked down, her stomach turned. The consulate building was tall and narrow, and the drop to the slate terrace below was frighteningly steep—an invitation to broken bones, or a broken neck.

Paco reached into the bushes and pulled out something that looked to Brigitte like a series of sheets that had been tied together. From her vantage point on the roof, she could see four lone pillowcases hanging on the line of the house next door. She looked down at Paco, who had the matching sheets tucked under his arm and was studying the walls of the building. He disappeared around a corner, and Brigitte hurried over to the edge of the roof and looked down in time to see him wedge one foot between a drainpipe and the wall. The pipe did not look sturdy enough to support a spider, much less a *saltimbanque*. Yet Paco was inching his way toward her, hoisting himself up, getting small purchases on the wall by clinging to the mortar spaces between the bricks. He scaled the side of the house as if he were a human fly.

When he stepped onto the roof, Brigitte flew to him. "Oh, Paco . . . I am so glad to see you! Pavlov has Romero! What if he sees us? How did you know where I was?" The words tumbled out of her in a rush.

Paco was panting, hands on knees, head down. "You didn't use your ticket for the performance tonight . . . and then I remembered you were delivering Pavlov's dinner. I put two and two together. Nothing keeps you away from the circus—and then I remembered how you answered my question about Pavlov yesterday. I knew you were up to something."

"I didn't lie! I just chose my words carefully. . . ."

Paco shook his head as if she were a naughty child, and Brigitte quickly changed the subject.

"Romero is an anarchist, Paco—a real one, not one who just talks! And Henri is helping him! I found a copy of a letter Monsieur Pavlov sent to the Sûreté Générale. It says terrible things! Pavlov has been watching everyone—including Picasso."

Paco collected himself. "The picture has fallen into place, but we have no time for explanations now. We have to get down."

Paco walked the perimeter of the roof, looking down over its edge. When he selected his spot, he spread out the bedsheets and tightened the knots that held them together, motioning Brigitte to his side with a hand gesture. "It's grass below, and there aren't many windows on this side of the house. Come, look. Could any of them be in the room where Pavlov and his friends are dining?"

Brigitte looked down, and when she did her head started to swim. A narrow grassy area lay below. The shape of the windows she saw were not like the ones in the room where the picnic had been laid out. "It looks all right. But how do we know where Pavlov is? He could be anywhere in the house."

Paco nodded grimly. "He could. But we must take a chance."

"How are we going to do this?" she asked, her voice catching in her throat.

"Didn't Anna Maria give you a turn on the Spanish web?" Paco replied. "Well, now you are going to have another chance to try that."

Paco walked to the drainage pipe. He shook it, and it moved easily.

"I don't like to use this for an anchor, but we have no choice," he said, knotting one end of the string of sheets around the pipe.

Brigitte watched in silence as Paco threw the homemade rig over the side of the building. It fell short of the ground by several feet.

"You're going to have a good drop when you get to the bottom," he said. "Just remember what I told you at the circus. Relax into the fall. You go first. I'll stay here to be certain this end stays secure."

Brigitte looked over the edge of the building. The knotted sheets hung limply down its side. Her body began to tremble. "I . . . I can't do this," she whispered. Her lips were stiff, and she struggled to shape the words.

"I thought you wanted to be in the circus," he said. "It's a simple enough trick. Pretend it's the Spanish web, and you're at the Medrano."

"But the Spanish web has loops for hands and feet!"

"Just hang onto the rope and climb down it. Whatever you do, don't loose your grip. And watch that you don't get tangled in your skirts."

Brigitte swallowed hard. She had wanted excitement and a chance to perform. But this? Could she do this? She sat down on the edge of the roof and swung one leg over, wrapping it around the soft sheets.

"Don't look down," Paco said. "Keep looking at me."

Brigitte reached out with one hand and grasped the sheet rope.

"Good," said Paco. "Now the other leg."

Brigitte wrapped her second leg around the sheets and felt the line give with the weight of her body. She stifled a small scream, and placed her other hand on it.

"You're on the web now, Brigitte. Keep looking here," Paco said. "Let yourself down—but hurry! Remember to relax into the fall at the bottom."

The sheets twisted of their own accord as Brigitte worked her way down, hand by hand, as quickly as she dared. She tried to keep her eyes on Paco, but as she neared the bottom, she looked down. It was at least a five-foot drop from the end of the rope to the terrace below. She took a deep breath, said a prayer, and relaxed into the fall.

Chapter 23

THE PLOT

"I THINK I GOT DOWN with little luck to spare," Paco said as he tugged on the sheet rope, and it fell to the ground at his feet. "I could feel the anchor knot coming loose." He tossed the sheets back into the neighbor's yard.

"I don't think we should take time to hang them back on the line," he said, allowing himself a small smile now that they were safely off the roof.

"Hurry! Come on!" Brigitte managed to answer.

They ran into the street, darting from shadow to shadow, fearing the Okhrana, waiting for the worst. Finally the pair darted into an alley and stopped.

"Paco, you said you would explain. . . ." Brigitte was leaning against a wall, waiting for her heart to stop slamming against her ribs, while marveling at the fact that all her bones seemed to be intact.

"Henri came to the circus tonight. He was distraught. He may have been drinking wine—I couldn't tell. But he was loud and he was brandishing the knife—"

"—the one he was taking to the tinker to be sharpened?"

"The same." Paco nodded. "You know how easily offended Henri is."

Brigitte nodded, urging him on.

"Well, tonight he was acting crazy. He said Picasso had refused his invitation to join his political party—I assume he made an overture to Picasso when he went to the studio to apologize."

"Oh, you know how Henri resented having to make that apology," Brigitte said, remembering the scene with Dominique in the kitchen.

"Yes," Paco agreed. "Henri's pride will get him in the end."

"And to think he had another rejection on top of the apology," Brigitte shuddered to think about Henri's mood after that.

"Indeed. I suspect Henri had been bragging about his so-called 'friendship' with Picasso, and Romero saw an opportunity to grow the membership of his cell. He said Romero had asked him to bring Picasso into the party." Paco shook his head. "So foolish, really. Picasso cares not a fig for political organizations. He just likes to talk about politics."

"Well, the Okhrana seem to think differently," Brigitte said, remembering the letter she had discovered in Pavlov's office.

Paco shrugged. "I gather the Okhrana suspect their own grandmothers of treason. Anyway, listen. Henri was so upset with Picasso that he said he was going to slash the painting—the one I pose for."

"But that painting is everything to Picasso!" Brigitte cried.

"Precisely. And that is why Henri is intent on destroying it. In the end, I had to make a decision. I could go to the studio and try to stop Henri, or—since Pavlov's name had come up in Henri's rant—I could come to see about your welfare. In the end, I chose a person over a painting."

Tired as she was, and not trusting herself—for once—to say a word, Brigitte managed a small smile. He had chosen her over a painting.

Finally, Paco took a cautious step into the street. "Come on!" he said, gesturing that Brigitte was to follow him.

"Where are we going?" she asked, thinking longingly of the small iron bed with its clean, fresh sheets waiting for her back at the café.

"To the Bateau-Lavoir. To check on Picasso's painting!"

Chapter 24

THE STUDIO

IT WAS NOT FAR to 13 Rue Ravignan and the ramshackle building known as the Bateau-Lavoir. Viewed from the front, the building appeared to be a one-story structure. However, Paco approached from the Rue Garaud, the street that ran behind the building. From that vantage point it was clear that the rickety wooden structure actually had five stories. To Brigitte, it looked as if all five floors were on the verge of collapse, as none of them were square to the ground and they leaned at precarious angles.

"This is the Bateau-Lavoir?" said Brigitte. "I thought it would be more . . . elegant."

Paco shrugged. "They have no money, remember? It is not so bad, really." He went into the building with the comfort of one who had been there often.

Unlike the more prosperous and newer buildings in Montmartre, the Bateau-Lavoir had not been fitted for gas service, so there were no tiny flames burning in wall sconces, as there were at the Russian consulate. Here the hallways were dark; the only light came from candles whose glow seeped through cracks in the wallboards that separated the various apartments and studios. Brigitte kept close to Paco as they moved through the dim and dirty hallways.

"Picasso's studio is on the ground floor," Paco said. "We entered the building on the fifth floor. We'll have to walk down to it."

The smells inside the building made Brigitte's stomach turn. Chamber pots had not been emptied, she guessed, for days. A dangerous bile rose in her throat, and she wished she had brought a handkerchief to hold to her nose. She glanced at Paco to see if he was as uncomfortable as she, but he seemed unaware of the stench. Brigitte's thoughts drifted to the tents at the Medrano. It was not so different there. *He must be used to it,* she thought.

Paco quickly led the way down narrow, twisting flights of stairs until they reached the first floor. Violin music came from one apartment, and the sounds of a couple arguing at the tops of their lungs came from another. It was numbingly cold inside, and Brigitte wondered how Picasso kept himself warm enough to paint. She rubbed her arms vigorously as she thought of the warmth of Dominique's kitchen.

"The studio is at the end of this hallway," Paco said.

Paco gave a rap on the door and waited. Picasso's two dogs barked furiously at the disturbance, and Brigitte jumped.

"That's just Fricka and Gat," Paco said. "They bark at a shadow."

When no one came to the door, Paco looked at Brigitte. "No one is here," he said. Brigitte swallowed hard, and took her place behind Paco. What if some-one—perhaps Henri—were in there?

"No one locks doors at the Bateau-Lavoir," Paco said, slowly pushing the studio door open. As Paco and Brigitte stepped inside, the dogs stopped barking and ran up to the familiar figure, eager to have their heads scratched. The smells of turpentine, stale cigarette smoke, linseed oil, and general dirt all came together in a scent that made Brigitte gag once again. Though it was dark, she was able to make out a small table, covered with newspaper. The remains of what had been a fried fish—it looked like a sardine—lay on top. They were alone in the studio, and Brigitte sighed with relief.

"No wonder Picasso likes to dine at the café," she said, as Paco struck a match and lit the candle that was also on the tabletop. The studio sprang into a dim light, and Brigitte could see ice crystals that had formed around the edges of an abandoned cup of tea.

"How do Picasso and Fernande bear this cold?" she asked.

"It is warmer when more people are in the studio," Paco replied. "And they are used to it, like me."

Brigitte took a step forward, and Paco restrained her arm.

"Mind that you watch for the dog droppings," he said.

Brigitte looked at the floor. Discarded tubes of paint mixed with the droppings from Fricka and Gat. The floor was littered with hazards.

"Fernande is not much on tidying up, is she?" Brigitte said.

Paco let out a small laugh. "No, she admits it. She doesn't like housework. And Picasso—he needs chaos in order to work. He has said so many times. Would you like to see his mouse?"

"Oh, I would!" Brigitte said. She had heard Picasso's *bande* talk of Picasso's pet mouse, which he kept in a drawer in his studio. Occasionally Fernande took a small piece of her cheese home to it.

Paco walked over to the table and opened a small drawer about a quarter of an inch. There was a quiver of whiskers and a flash of fur. Then a curious pointy face with eyes almost as black as the painter's looked directly at Brigitte.

"Cunning!" she said. "May I hold him?"

"There's no time for that," Paco said, his voice sharp. "Something is very wrong here."

"What's wrong?"

"Look around. The paintings are gone."

Brigitte looked toward the easel that was set up in the center of the room. It was empty. A few canvases leaned against the walls, and Brigitte hurried to them.

"Those are not Picasso's work," Paco said. "He often buys poor-quality paintings from junk dealers, just to get the canvas."

Brigitte looked at one. "Isn't this a Picasso?" she said.

Paco was impatient. "That's just a study. He hasn't begun to finish it. I tell you, his paintings are not here— not the ones he cares about, anyway. And my painting is missing! We're too late. Henri has done his damage."

"Do you think Henri has stolen them?" Brigitte asked. "But he was only going to destroy one painting."

"I know. I thought he was only going to slash the *saltimbanques* . . . and that was terrible enough. But he must have taken them all—cut them into ribbons and stuffed them in the sewer, or . . ." Paco sat in a small chair and buried his head in his arms. "All that work . . . the months of it. Gone."

"It can't be," said Brigitte. She ran to the back of the studio, determined to look everywhere. There was a mattress on the floor, in a kind of sleeping alcove set off from the rest of the studio by a velvet curtain.

"Paco, what is this tableau?" Brigitte asked, pointing to something that looked curiously like an altar in a cathedral.

Paco came into the area and smiled ruefully. "It's his homage to the love he shares with Fernande." Paco lifted the red cloth that covered the table. "See, it's really a packing crate."

Paco let the cloth drop back into place and picked up a picture of Fernande that was displayed on top. "At least Picasso will still have this piece. It's a sketch he drew of her, right after they met. And the blouse that you see here, well, that is the blouse Fernande was wearing on that day. It was raining."

"I have heard her tell that story at the café," Brigitte said, gazing at the crumpled blouse, so carefully placed. "See, he has placed a red rose on it." Brigitte took in the scene—the portrait, the blouse, the faded rose, and the blue vase with artificial flowers in it. She sighed. Someday she would like to be loved like that.

Her thoughts were interrupted by raucous laughter and gunshots that sounded as if they were being fired into the air.

"Someone has a gun!" she said to Paco, terrified.

"Long live Rimbaud!" came a voice from the street. "The greatest of the French poets!"

"That's Apollinaire yelling," Paco said. "Picasso never leaves the Bateau-Lavoir at night without carrying his gun. Obviously, the *bande à Picasso* has been having a literary discussion."

"And he feels that he has to accent his discussion with a gunshot?" Brigitte said.

Paco shrugged. "He means no harm. He's had too much wine at the café."

"Well, their discussion has deteriorated into something else," said Brigitte. "We need to leave. I . . . we . . . can't be caught in his studio. How will we explain it? What if he thinks we took the paintings? What . . . what if he shoots us?" Brigitte felt a return of the terror she had felt earlier in the evening.

At the sound of Picasso's voice, the dogs sent up a terrible racket, barking and yelping in excited anticipation. The noise covered the sound of Paco and Brigitte running from the studio and up the narrow staircase. Just as they escaped into the safety of Rue Garaud, Picasso and his party entered the Bateau-Lavoir from the Rue Ravignan. By the time they reached the studio, Paco and Brigitte were two blocks away.

Chapter 25

THE PAINTINGS

IT WAS QUITE LATE by the time Brigitte returned to the Café Dominique. She was cold to the bone, exhausted from the night's activities, and sad at the thought of Picasso's missing paintings—and suddenly terrified as she contemplated facing her aunt. To her astonishment, she found a note from Dominique, lying in the center of the butcher block in the kitchen.

I would have waited up for you, my dear, but I have been taken with a terrible headache and Georges insisted we go to bed. He says you can take care of yourself. In the morning, plan to tell me every detail about Monsieur Pavlov's dinner party. It must have gone on quite late. I do hope you enjoyed the circus and had a pleasant evening.

Exhausted as she was, the note made Brigitte smile. A pleasant evening, indeed. Brigitte climbed the steps as quietly as possible, and fell asleep as soon as her head settled on the goose feather pillow. She slept hard all night long, until she was awakened by the sound of her aunt's voice.

"Georges, I cannot believe it, but Henri is late yet again. I am at my wit's end with that boy. Now I have to go to Andre's farm. I failed to get enough eggs for today's quiches."

Brigitte threw on her clothes and hurried down the stairs. "I'll go for you, Aunt," she said, trying to shake off the weariness that made her feel as if her brain had been wrapped in a cobweb. She used the kitchen pump and splashed cold water onto her face to shock it awake.

Dominique smiled at her niece. "You're up so early! Since you worked so hard at Monsieur Pavlov's dinner party, and then went to the circus, I was going to let you sleep for a while."

Guilt rose in Brigitte. Her poor aunt! Little did she know what her niece had been up to in the middle of the night. Secret police, daring escapes, visits to bohemian studios . . . In an excess of eagerness, she replied, "I don't mind, Aunt. Honestly, I don't. Just let me go. How many eggs do you need—one, two dozen?"

"Well, if you're sure, then. Two dozen should be

enough," said Dominique, rummaging in her purse for the necessary coins. "Tell Andre I want his very freshest ones. If they were laid this morning, that would be best."

"I'll tell him," said Brigitte, throwing on her cloak and hurrying out the back door of the café. Before she got out the door, Dominique called to her.

"Oh, Brigitte, before I forget to tell you—guess what I read in today's paper? Our young friend, Picasso, is actually having an exhibit of his paintings. Of course, it's just at a furniture store, but still . . . an exhibit is an accomplishment."

Brigitte stopped in her tracks. "Picasso? An exhibit? Where?"

"The Galeries Serrurier."

Brigitte knew the store. The owner sold furniture and, occasionally, art. "Oh, Aunt Dominique!" she cried emotionally, throwing her arms around the startled woman.

"There, there, my little one," said Dominique, patting her awkwardly. "I didn't know you were so interested in art! Why don't you stop by there on your way back with the eggs? It is not far from Andre's."

"I won't take long, but I believe I will pass by the store if you don't mind. Thank you, Aunt!" Brigitte said to the bewildered Dominique as she flew out the door, heading first to Andre's for the eggs, then to the store.

Brigitte stood outside for a moment, studying the sign that hung above her: "Galeries Serrurier: Furnishings and Artistic Décor."

Next her eyes fell to a poster that was propped in a corner of the display window. It announced a new exhibition of works by various local artists. Her eye scanned up and down, and finally she saw the name she was looking for—Pablo Picasso. Not daring to hope, Brigitte stared through the window, cupping her hands by the side of her face to block out the morning sun, which was now well up in the February sky. She was desperately trying to catch a glimpse of a Picasso . . . any Picasso. But she saw nothing.

She tried the door, not expecting it to be open this early, but to her surprise it swung inward, and she stepped inside. Signs saying "Exhibition" led her to a back room where the paintings were on display. Many were signed simply "Picasso" in the lower right-hand corner. Brigitte's heart jumped with excitement. Could these be the missing paintings? If she found the *saltimbanque* painting, she would know with certainty.

The first piece she saw was a pen-and-charcoal drawing, not more than a sketch, really, that depicted an acrobat's family—the mother holding a baby while the father looked on. A dog stood between the adults. Brigitte studied the piece and thought she recognized the family. One of the lady acrobats had given birth to a baby in the past month, and Brigitte had come upon Picasso apparently admiring the child. She wondered if this was the sketch he had done on the spot, or if he remembered the family and re-created them in his studio.

As she walked through the rest of the exhibit, Brigitte was struck with the color that seemed to be common to each of them—a kind of dull rose shade, almost terra-cotta. *Aunt Dominique would be happy*, she thought; *Picasso is using a color other than blue.*

A young girl on a balance ball, supervised by a trainer, caught her eye. She thought, *That looks like one of the Vela sisters. And the trainer is the image of Lars.* The trainer seemed to dominate the young girl, as Lars dominated members of the Cirque Medrano. In the background, Picasso had painted a mother, a dog, and two children. In the distance on the barren plain, there was Miss La La's white horse. But where was the masterpiece? Had Henri destroyed it after all?

A man approached her. "I see you admire the *saltimbanques*—and so early in the morning," he said. "May I offer you a catalog of the exhibit? The circus paintings are the work of a young artist by the name of Picasso. Pablo Picasso. My name is Charles Morice. I work here."

Brigitte, feeling silly for carrying a basket of eggs to

an art exhibit, accepted the catalog and began to explain why she had arrived so early.

"I had to get eggs for my aunt, Dominique Boudoin. She owns the Café Dominique. Picasso comes there and—and I heard of the exhibit and wanted to stop in."

Morice looked at her with a bemused expression, and Brigitte plowed on.

"I have heard about one painting—it is quite large, I think—of an entire family of *saltimbanques*, but I don't see it. Is it here?" Her heart pounded as she waited for his reply.

He nodded his head slowly. "Ahhh . . . *Family of Saltimbanques*. But of course it is here. As you said, it is large—so large it required a space of its own. Follow me," he said, leading Brigitte around the corner and into another small room where, displayed in solitary splendor, was *Family of Saltimbanques*.

At the sight of it, Brigitte drew in her breath. The canvas was enormous, much taller than she was, at least seven feet by eight feet. Gazing at it, Brigitte was overwhelmed with a melancholy feeling, and she wasn't certain whether she brought the feeling to the painting, or the painting evoked the feeling in her. Still, for some inexplicable reason, her eyes filled with tears as she looked at the six figures and the lonely landscape.

Morice noticed her reaction to the art. "You sense

the isolation," he said softly. "Picasso has captured the loneliness of these people well, has he not?"

Brigitte nodded, not trusting herself to speak.

"Did you see that Picasso has painted himself in this work? See—he is there. The harlequin on the left. And the large jester? His friend, Apollinaire."

"Yes," said Brigitte. "I see him. I see them all. The rest are members of a circus family I know," Brigitte told Morice. "The *saltimbanque* holding a knapsack is called Paco; his little brother, next to him, is Manuel—see how his clothes are too big for him? They are hand-me-downs from Paco. And the girl with her back to us and her head down, she is Anna Maria, their sister. See the arm that rests on the flowers? She hurt it in a fall."

"And the woman with the water jug?" asked Morice.

Brigitte took a closer look. "It could be Fernande, I don't know. No matter who she is, she is full of sadness."

Morice stood back, studying the canvas. "Sad. Hmmmm. Well, I would say Picasso is describing a condition, more than stating an emotion, in this painting."

"Then I think their condition is sad," said Brigitte, not willing to have her own interpretation taken away from her. "They are wanderers, and they have no home. What could be sadder than that?"

With the mention of the word "home," thoughts of

the Café Dominique flew into Brigitte's head. She longed to be there, safe and warm. "I must go," she said. "My aunt is waiting for these eggs."

Morice accompanied Brigitte to the door. "The exhibit remains open until March sixth. Please tell people about it. The poor artist needs to sell something," he said.

"Oh, I'll tell people," Brigitte answered. "I'll be certain to do that."

⁕

Picasso's paintings were safe! Brigitte could hardly wait to share the news with Paco. She calculated her time. The Medrano was only a short detour away, and she hurried in its direction.

When she arrived at the circus, she bypassed the pink tent and made her way among the performers' tents to the place where Paco's family had pitched theirs. To her surprise, it was collapsed. Paco was packing things into a knapsack as a tearful Anna Maria handed items to him. Toulouse sat nearby, tethered to a stake in the ground.

"What are you doing?" Brigitte demanded, surprising both of them with the harshness of her tone.

Paco looked up for a moment, then went back to packing. "I'm sorry, Brigitte. We're leaving," he said simply.

"Just like that?" Brigitte did not trust herself to say more.

"Lars fired us," said Anna Maria. "I can't perform anymore—not even on the web. My arm is too sore. And little Manuel is too sick to go on with any training. He coughs and can't keep much food down."

"Just as well, since we have little food to spare," Paco said, tossing a tin cup into the knapsack.

"Isn't that the monkey's cup?" Brigitte asked.

Paco smiled. "So it is. He won't be needing it."

Dread filled Brigitte's heart. "Paco!"

"Don't worry. I'm not going to leave him here for Lars to shoot. He is going to Picasso. He has a fondness for animals, and he likes Toulouse."

"Then I'll be able to see him from time to time."

"If Dominique allows the creature into the café," Paco said.

"Oh, I think I can prevail upon her," said Brigitte. Hot tears were stinging her eyes. "I'm so sorry you are leaving, Paco."

"We're *saltimbanques*," he replied. "Nothing is ever permanent for us. Picasso has told me of a circus in Barcelona. We're going there."

"Oh, Paco—I have wonderful news!" she said, remembering why she had come. "Your painting is safe!"

"I know," Paco replied. "I risked the painter's wrath by going by the studio this morning—to inquire about bringing the monkey there, and to say good-bye," he said. "Picasso told me about the exhibit. Who knows? Perhaps something will sell. He has hopes."

"I saw the painting. It's wonderful, a masterpiece," Brigitte said quickly. Then, more quietly, "To think what Henri could have done . . ."

"Perhaps. But it was another in his list of failures. If he made it to the studio, he found it as empty as we did."

"What do you suppose Henri really wants?" Brigitte asked.

Paco shook his head. "I think he is trying to figure that out."

"Do you think he really would have destroyed the painting? What good would that do anyone?"

Paco shrugged his shoulders. "Anger makes people do many stupid things, and Henri seems angry most of the time. His temper gets the better of him; he acts, and then he thinks."

"And he should think, and then act," Brigitte said, knowing as soon as the words formed that she sounded exactly like her mother.

Paco nodded. "Henri wants change in Russia. Last night, during his outburst, he said he was going there to join those who want to achieve that change with violence, and that is—"

"—wrong," Brigitte finished the sentence. "Uncle

Georges says people should be mindful of what they are for, as much as what they are against. He says being for things brings—what did he call it—reformation. Being against things brings revolution."

"An interesting concept," Paco said, throwing his knapsack on the back of a cart. "Henri is against the tsars, but it is unclear what he would replace them with. Perhaps one day we will see."

Anna Maria moved next to Brigitte, clutching something in her hand. It was the faded red rose she wore in her hair when she performed. "Here, I want you to have this," she said softly. "To remember me."

"I will always remember you, Anna Maria," Brigitte said, suddenly stooping to give the child a kiss on the cheek. "Be a good girl," she said. "No more stealing apples—promise?"

Anna Maria remained silent. *She probably doesn't want to lie to me,* Brigitte thought, feeling certain that Anna Maria had not "borrowed" her last apple.

She looked from Paco to Anna Maria and sighed. "I cannot linger. Dominique is waiting for these eggs and I need to go . . . home." There. The word just slipped out of her lips, surprising herself with the sweetness of its sound. "Just remember . . ." She exchanged a long last look with Paco and Anna Maria.

"What? Remember what?" Anna Maria said eagerly, as if Brigitte was going to invoke some kind of magic spell that would make the departure unnecessary.

Brigitte smiled at the child and waited until the sudden ache in her throat subsided. "Remember . . . whenever you are in Paris, you are always welcome at the Café Dominique."

When Brigitte slipped into the kitchen, a pot of water simmered on top of the stove and pie crusts were already in their pans, the edges crimped attractively, waiting for quiche custard to be poured into them. Georges was standing by the butcher block, turning Dominique's carving knife over and over in his hand. "I found this lying on the back stoop this morning," he said, pausing to examine it closely. "Odd. Dominique always believes in putting things in their proper place."

"Henri was going to take it to the tinker's for sharpening," Brigitte said.

"Yes . . . I heard," Georges said slowly. "He hasn't come to work today—and I doubt we will see him again. I suspect it was he who left the knife."

"I wish I could have said goodbye," Brigitte said.

Georges looked at his niece. "It might have been good practice for him, my dear. I fear that Henri will face many farewells along the path he has chosen. Your aunt has gone to Sacré Coeur to say a small prayer."

Brigitte went into the kitchen and surveyed the scene there. She twisted her braid up on her head and pinned it there with Anna Maria's rose. Then she took a fresh apron and tied it around herself. She began to crack the eggs into a bowl, practicing the art of doing so with one hand. The work of a café went on, and people needed to be fed.

Shortly, Dominique returned from Mass. She watched as Brigitte carefully poured the custard into the pastry shells. "I could not run this café without you, my dear," she said. Brigitte looked at the glint in her aunt's eyes. Were those tears?

She smiled. "I love helping you," she said simply. "I love living my life here, with you, and Uncle Georges. And Aunt—I saw the exhibit! Picasso is . . ."

"Picasso!" exclaimed her aunt. "Did I tell you he has started working in pen and ink?"

"Another art form!" said Brigitte. "He certainly is versatile."

"On my napkins, Brigitte! On my napkins!"

Brigitte laughed. "Give them to me. I'll wash them for you."

Author's Note

Picasso once said, "A picture lives only through the one who looks at it. And what they see is the legend surrounding the picture." *Secrets of the Cirque Medrano* is the story I created around a legend I imagined when I looked at *Family of Saltimbanques*, Picasso's masterpiece from his Rose Period. While the characters of Brigitte, Henri, Paco, Anna Maria, Dominique, Georges, and Pavlov are fictional (though quite real to me), like any legend, this story contains some truth.

It is true that at the turn of the twentieth century, Montmartre was still a hilly village on the outskirts of Paris, full of cafés, narrow dirt streets, vineyards and windmills. The area attracted the avant-garde, those who were inventing and applying the new ideas of their time. This group included writers, artists, bohemians, and revolutionaries—especially those interested in overturning tsarist Russia. This was the Montmartre of Picasso and his friends—Guillaume Apollinaire, Max Jacob, and the beautiful Fernande Olivier. Their lives and their work were influenced by this culture.

It is true that Picasso's friends were devoted to him, praised his work, and often wrote about it. In the case of Apollinaire, the quote that begins, "One feels that his slender acrobats . . . are . . . dexterous, poverty-stricken, and lying" comes from a critique that Apollinaire wrote about the Galeries Surrurier exhibit. Apollinaire's review appeared in *La Plume* (May 15, 1905) after the exhibit closed. As a writer, I allowed myself the luxury of imagining that Apollinaire would have formed that opinion as he watched the painting take form in Picasso's studio, so I took the liberty of moving the quote to a time before the exhibit opened, instead of after it closed.

It is true that the Okhrana—the Russian Imperialist Secret Police—established themselves at the Russian consulate at 97 Rue de Grenelle during this time. The Okhrana were masterminds of counter-espionage, and in fact, are given credit for raising that spy technique to an art form. They were the fore-runners of the Russian KGB, an organization that continues to function today as the FSB. The Okhrana had Picasso and his friends under observation, though there is no evidence that Picasso ever participated in revolutionary activities. He did join the Communist Party later in his life.

It is true that the Cirque Medrano was housed in a pink tent at the foot of the Montmartre bluff and featured the kinds of performances described in the book. Picasso and his band of friends frequently visited there, and Picasso drew inspiration from the performances. Circus life was brutal, but Lars and Romero are fictional characters.

Picasso's rickety studio, the Bateau-Lavoir, actually stood at 13 Rue de Ravignon. Picasso and Fernande, along with the tame mouse and the dogs, Fricka and Gat, made their home there. During this time, the couple was frequently hungry, and at times Picasso traded a painting for food or art supplies. New canvases were expensive, and he often visited junk shops in order to purchase inferior work from other artists, just to have the canvas to paint over. Despite the squalor of his studio, the freezing weather in winter, and the stifling heat in summer, in his later years Picasso once said he had spent the happiest days of his life living at the Bateau-Lavoir.

Picasso drew constantly—at the circus, in a café, even in the dirt for the amusement of neighborhood children. He drew on anything that was available to him—dirt, paper, canvas, napkins—it didn't seem to matter. The need to draw, to express his perspective on life, continued until his death.

Art historians have described the figures in *Family of Saltimbanques* as Picasso in the harlequin suit, Apollinaire as the jester dressed in red, and Max Jacob as the *saltimbanque* with the kit on his back. The art historians seem less certain about the other figures—the two younger children and the woman who sits apart from the group, though there is speculation that the woman could be Fernande and the young girl could be either a Montmartre child who modeled for Picasso, or a young girl Fernande may have adopted for a short time. To me, of course, the young girl is Anna Maria, and the boy with the kit on his back is Paco. The young boy is their little brother, Manuel. And the woman staring into the distance, contemplating yet another move, is their mother.

"A picture lives only through the one who looks at it."

This story is how *Family of Saltimbanques* lives through me. When you look at the art, it could tell you a different story and therefore have an entirely different life.

Family of Saltimbanques now hangs in the National Gallery of Art in Washington, D.C.